An Apartment In Madrid

Copyright © 2013 - Margaret Prezioso-Frye

ISBN:978-1-4689-2415-2 Booktango / Booktango.com

CONTENTS:

To:

My children, Amber and Seth, who both have been and continue to be inspirations in my life, and Sylas, a brand new grandchild who looks like his Grandma.

And

My students whom I regaled with tales of trying to find an apartment in Madrid with all the outrageous events that accompanied them. They kept saying to me, "you should write a book" and they meant it. Thanks for the push that ignited a spark, and gave me a groove. Through all the exhaustion once again, here it is. As for Madrid, I can recommend the jamon.

Forward (Always)

It wasn't easy rehashing the events of thirteen months of living in Madrid. You could say it's because thirteen is unlucky, but I know it's not. My daughter was born November thirteenth at three-thirteen in the morning, so thirteen is fine with me. (I can hear my son say, "Ma, you didn't mention my birthday." He's my Thanksgiving baby, born during dinnertime.) Besides that, one and three add to four, which is a good number according to feng shui. During this time I managed to: fulfill all obligations to the schools I worked for, survive all those who changed their mind therefore changing my life as I knew it when I least expected it, and get to know the city so well I could work as a tour guide. Would I go back to be a tour guide? No, but there's great shopping.

I'd never would've thought of writing a book about any of it, but I used my comedies of error as English lessons often enough that my three advanced students were adamant I do this. Whether for therapy or lusty entertainment, when I realized they were dead serious, I re-embarked on my journey, my "Spanish Adventure" doubting I'd come up with anything worthwhile. Part of me dreaded recalling where I'd been and I mentally whined, "I don't like this". I relived it: success, surprise, pain, stress, exhaustion and relief. Each time I read the manuscript - I can't believe I said manuscript - I recalled another detail. Many times I wanted the details to stop but they didn't and here we are. There are days I'd still just as soon forget about it, but through thick and thin Madrid has become a part of me now. We're family, sometimes dysfunctional, but as good as any family around.

The link for the school that got my attention and tripped me down the rabbit hole claimed, "Teach in Madrid, Spain! Your Spanish Adventure awaits you!" Never did I envision adventure to be like this.

Prologue: A McGuffin Italiano

I thought it would be cool...

I'd been working in Italy and absolutely loved my job. I came back to the States with a stack of paperwork to get my working permit and the Consulate flat out said no, "this is a contract for EU citizens. ARE YOU AN EU CITIZEN?" Devastated I muttered, "My life is there." The attendant became momentarily tender and softly said, "I know." I know? How did he know? After trying to figure out a way back in as a year ticked by, I spotted an ad online that said: "Teach in Madrid Spain! Your Spanish Adventure Awaits." I'd never considered Spain for much of anything; in fact, just recently I'd been searching for jobs in Croatia inspired by my son who'd taken a vacation there. "It's awesome", he'd said. "Ma, I could live there." Sounded good to me. Itching to get back to what I'd been doing - teaching and traveling - I contacted the school. I've made this same mistake with my husbands, now my ex-husbands. Neither of them were my type exactly, not really what I was looking for, but they kept presenting themselves like that link to teach in Madrid did, no matter what I looked up it was on the page, so I gave them a try.

I composed my first email to the school…

Chapter 1: How Do I Get Myself Into These Things?

"Come to Madrid!" the ad said. "Your Spanish adventure awaits you." But I wasn't looking to teach in Madrid, in fact, I'd never been interested in Spain, if it's possible you can imagine there's someone on the planet not interested in seeing Spain. I was looking for a job in Croatia inspired by my son who'd gone for a vacation. "It's awesome," he'd said. "Ma, I could live there." Sounded good to me. To my annoyance the link for the school in Madrid kept populating and the information I wanted about Croatia didn't. I don't give up and neither did the link. After a couple weeks of unsuccessful searching I decided to contact the school. I've made this same mistake choosing my husbands, now ex-husbands. They weren't my type exactly, not really what I was interested in but they kept crossing my path so each respective time I thought, "well, why not?" As I composed my first fateful email to send I thought, "well, why not Spain...could be interesting." This wasn't going to be my first international teaching position; I began teaching in foreign countries in 2006.

The wheels for overseas adventure started turning while my daughter was still living at home; my son had traveled to Italy to attend a university and I had my very first European vacation when I visited him. My then 19-year-old daughter decided to stay home to have our apartment to herself, if you can imagine someone refusing a vacation in Italy; wonder where she gets that. (What I had to deal with when I returned home is another story, which I think I'll title, "The Checkbook."). Anyway, when I saw the town it was love at first sight; I knew I could live there, work there and be happy. A few months after she decided to move out that spark burst back into flame.

It happened during homework for my Master's one afternoon, the thought kept creeping into my head I didn't have to stay where I was. I'm a single mom after all, the kids are grown and now both were gone. At first I mused, "What do I want to do with my life?" and then reality hit. I became giddy as if I were taking long awaited sips from the fountain of youth and thought "Huh. What do I want to do? I don't have to stay. I don't have to stay..." I decided to take the advice I'd given my kids as they were growing: unless you are absolutely positive you aren't good at it - try everything, travel, and check the world out. We're a European - genuine American combo: mom's family is Italian and dad's is an American Indian, British and Swiss mix, all which equal homes in other places to explore, domestic and export! I'd been substitute teaching while working on my degree and though new to the profession, decided then and there to try my hand at teaching abroad.

I started searching for places that certified teachers for TEFL, a four week intensive course designed to verify, certify, and give polish to your credentials while promising to fling wide open doors of opportunity for positions. The one I decided on had schools all over Europe, so I selected Rome as my first choice and Bordeaux as my second. I was contacted by a school in Rome and made plans with them to take the course after I graduated. When I got my degree, I gave notice and off I went! After a stellar month (Rome is fabulous), I went to Istanbul to visit my son who'd taken a detour from Italy to teach in Turkey and was hired within two days by a private language academy opening a branch nearby. As it turned out I lived in Istanbul for eight months and worked for three different schools. From there I traveled to northern Italy, to the very town that'd stolen my heart, and was hired by another language school. From Italy I came back to the U.S. with very high hopes for a work permit and languished over a year waiting for the paperwork that every official assured me I wasn't going to get. According to the consulate I had the wrong contract and the contract I needed, as an American, was next to impossible to get; there were a limited number of them permitted each year. As time ticked away, I became restless to get back to what I'd gotten myself into so, teaching English in Croatia turned into a barrage of questions for the school in Madrid. After all, I'd felt I'd been around. What I didn't know I didn't know!

My first question, would the school be interested in helping someone not taking their course but already TEFL certified, got an emphatic yes response with instructions to a link on their website. After scrutinization, I added a few specific queries along with what I'd learned to ask when considering a teaching job in a foreign country. My questions about volume of work, Spanish lessons, housing, what the government'd think of my presence there, will I need paperwork, what kind and so on were all answered satisfactorily. I was given options for what I could do when I arrived and was told I had to have a plane ticket to confirm my arrival date so everything could be finalized. I bought a ticket, filled out an application for housing, chose a room, chose taxi over metro - the subway as we say in the U.S. - to accommodate my inevitable jet-lag and as the school's internet brochure claimed, I set off on my "awaiting Spanish adventure".

Chapter 2: The Flamenco

I was told my new residence was located on a very famous Paseo. I didn't know the difference between a paseo and a calle yet, but it was famous. Beatriz, the woman I'd be sharing the apartment with and who'd also be my new landlady would be awaiting my arrival.

I landed at Barajas Airport, Madrid, found my way to the taxi stand and a taxi pulled into place. As we drove away down a modern highway and then exited to a wide super boulevard, my heart began to sink. My famous paseo was in a modern part of the city. I was harboring the desire that famous meant classic, always loving the atmosphere and architecture of older, classic European areas. I felt a familiar pang of disappointment as the cab stopped in front of the apartment building that was now my home. I thought of my first evening in Rome and how I'd felt when my taxi pulled up in front of a modern city building, the old Rome I'd envisioned nowhere in sight. Picking up on my disappointment that was steadily working its way to devastation, I was assured by the driver the place I was staying was really in Rome. He kept saying "Si! Si! Roma!" and went as far as getting out of the cab to ring the apartment for me all the while giving smiles of encouragement. As I unpacked tears began to fall. I sent an sms to my son telling him, "I am in hell. This isn't Rome. It's Italian NYC. Where's Rome?" It didn't make me any happier but it was better for me this time around I had no concept of Madrid.

The cab driver got my things as far as the elevator and from there I was on my own. I found the apartment and met Beatriz. The apartment was a lot smaller than the photos'd suggested. Experience and a bit of sense prepared me for what came next. My bedroom was smaller than most walk-in closets I've seen. In it was a small wardrobe with two racks that faced front instead of a rod running side to side, which meant I'd have to stagger hangers so clothes'd fit in and all that I wanted to hang up wouldn't be fitting in. There was a large dresser partially occupied with Beatriz' household items, table linens, and sheets for *her* bed. Outside my window that opened to a courtyard of walls and more windows, was a clothesline the length of the window directly under it. The bed at least was a regular twin size and there was just enough aisle space to walk between it and the dresser to get out the door to the bathroom. "All this for four hundred and fifty euro a month plus deposit", ran through my mind. I began to wonder just how expensive it was to live in Madrid and then considered it wasn't as expensive as New York City. Four-hundred and fifty euro roughly translated into seven-hundred U.S. dollars and I don't think there's a room for seven-hundred anywhere you wouldn't have to arm-wrestle cockroaches for in New York.

The second thing that struck me was Beatriz. Although she seemed nice enough, the way she acted after our initial meeting was odd. I mean, I expected cultural differences, but this threw me. After getting my keys and being given instructions on how to lock and unlock the front door, she changed to go out for a while. The shirt she'd decided to wear looked similar to one I had bought in Istanbul. (In fact, that similar cornflower blue shirt was packed in my suitcase.) It took only a few seconds for me to register all this but she didn't miss a beat that I was looking at her, reacted as if I were a man admiring her and my admiration was something that was expected; although she is a frumpier version of me around the same age, with serious effort and attention to detail I can boast the remnant of a waistline. I got a distinct of-course-you-think-I'm-beautiful vibe as she nodded toward me and broke into a knowing smile. Jet lag won over any further thought quickly quelling the lingering air of someone-had-smoked-in-her-room-not-too-long-ago that I'd also detected. On my application I'd selected to share with a non-smoker. I dropped it, went out for a while to look around, introduce myself at the school and tire myself out.

After that, things were fine for about a week, a week and a half. I kept detecting the lingering cigarette air but it was minimal. Beatriz let me know she used to dance the Flamenco, proudly pointing out portraits of her sketched by local artists hanging in the living room. Again I got that same vibe that she expected my admiration; that's what it was, she was prepared for it.

Now that I can reflect back on my experience of getting to know Madrileño women, I've come to realize that vibe was no more than vaingloriousness; a big unfriendly word, although originally I wanted to call it vaingloriosity to make the condition sound a bit more monstrous. Why? Many women of Madrid are overly competitive and centered on appearance. There's no sisterhood among them, no shared oneness woman to woman, which caused me many times to wonder how they made friends with each other at all. In the year I was there, the closest I'd seen to a sisterhood was the bond among prostitutes and transvestites of which there are many. Don't get me wrong, other professional business women do exist, chemists, biologists, plant managers, some of who I've had the privilege to teach and it is for them I add this. Sadly, there are a pronounced number who are the opposite. Being raised primarily in Italian culture, traditionally little girls through grown women shared a common bond. There were no secrets between us. I'm not speaking of gossipy clucking about personal business. We had a bond as women as we were growing, learning and knowing what it means, this intimacy of being a woman; it was in this ever-unfolding awareness we shared pains and joys. What I was experiencing was very different. Even after the jet lag wore off, I just wasn't into the adulation. Expecting laud and honor took away from the natural excitement I could've felt living with an actual celebrity. Be the situation as it may, little did I know my first Spanish adventure hadn't really taken off yet. In another week's time it was going to soar.

Chapter 3: Will the Real Beatriz Please Stand Up!

Within about a week's time after my arrival, when I stopped by the school to use the internet one morning, I met a teacher, a nurse from Holland, who was one of their TEFL alumni. We hit it off on the spot carrying on very lively conversation during which she asked where I was living. When I told her about Beatriz and mentioned little things I was noticing, her expression changed to furrowed concern and her voice dropped a couple of octaves to seriousness, "I used to live there. I asked to be moved to another flat because Beatriz was so horrible towards me. She doesn't like foreigners in her home." She paused for a second as if she were afraid to go on and was considering maybe she shouldn't have said that. I was momentarily stumped and confused as my mind tried to rationalize why I was given the offer to live there. Nothing too severe had happened and it didn't make sense the school would put another teacher in the same predicament, especially when it'd been made clear foreigners weren't welcomed. "Have you met her boyfriend Franco yet?", she asked. When I said no she assured me I wouldn't be spared the encounter. "Oh, you'll meet him. Have you met her friend she plays cards with yet?", she continued. "When they get together they both smoke so much the apartment is completely filled with it; you won't be able to breathe, believe me." I considered because she had complained and asked to be moved Beatriz, maybe, was trying to reform herself, but she continued on. " I couldn't wash my own clothes. She insisted on washing them for me. My showers were too long and always at the wrong time. It seemed I was always in the way of the student who lives in the other room. Have you met him yet? He's special to her for some reason; he's not family as far as I know. She gave me a hard time about so many things, when I accidentally broke a bowl I was afraid to tell her about it; I did tell her and she said it was ok, but I don't think she meant it. I had to eat my meals in my room. Does she make you eat in your room? And, no TV either. I wasn't allowed to watch TV past nine o'clock, she didn't want the noise, but the student could stay up as late as he liked. Did she tell you that? He can make all the noise he wants."

Having been a medical professional myself, I take pride in being able to remain serene under all circumstances in all emergencies, but I have to admit as I listened I felt like a dopey mutt with it's floppy ears raised and head cocked to one side with a big, "huh?" pasted on its face. I might have even had one limp paw up; hopefully my jaw hadn't dropped. I had to ask her, after this earful, how long ago she had lived at Beatriz'. She'd moved out only one week before I'd moved in; one week, only one week before.

I left the school with my mind reeling; this wasn't exactly someting I wanted to hear being in a different country so far from friends and family; however, I'd taught my kids not to base what you think of someone on what others say, base it on your experience firsthand: I hadn't met the student yet, had no idea someone else lived in the other room, but it was true I wasn't allowed to watch TV past nine. Beatriz'd said she'd do the laundry but I'd thought it was just a welcoming gesture of hospitality on her part. I did eat in my room, not at the table in the living room like she did; however, I didn't think anything of that, I was more than willing to give my hostess her privacy. I took my showers at odd times when no one was usually home not to be in the way, so the length of them went undetected. I brushed off the problem concluding that it'd been between Beatriz and the teacher; that was all I was going to handle right now. That bit of arrogance was going to cost me sooner than I knew.

I returned home. As I stood outside the apartment door turning the key the required three times to unlock and open it, I became aware of the strong smell of stale cigarette smoke that'd permeated the hallway. I instantly had a flashback of high school days, smoking in the girlsrooms, sitting on the bathroom floor against the wall in an effort to be cool about it although I didn't smoke, the taste in the back of my throat from smoky air and flushed toilets, and the hallways with a sickly lingering aroma that got stronger when the bell rang and we poured out in a sprint to our lockers and class. I stepped inside and thought in disbelief, "no way!" There was Beatriz and her friend sitting at the table, playing cards, drinking cerveza, (beer as we know it) and smoking like a couple of fired-up chimneys. Smoking! I knew I'd requested non-smoker on the application; I had a copy with me. The first thing I did when I made it to my room was check my paperwork in case I had selected the wrong square when I was filling it out, or there was a glitch that changed my input when I hit send.

Chapter 4: We Aye-Aye`t. It`s All Good in the Barrio

It must've been the look on my face that broke up the card game although it was obvious they'd been playing for a while. I glanced around, with equal amounts of distress and amazement in my expression, at smoke billowed everywhere. I looked back at them keeping my lips pursed, nodded a hello toward the guest, shifted my gaze back to Beatriz and headed for my room. When I came out again to go to the kitchen they were in the process of getting the living room organized and aired. All I could think was, "interesting"; they were behaving like a couple of kids who'd been caught at something. Beatriz looked at me and back to her friend mumbling Spanish under her breath. As I was cooking, the two of them came into the kitchen still mumbling to each other, then turned to look at me. Beatriz introduced her and both apologized for the smoke. I was assured they only smoked when they played cards and it was only once a week. "Interesting. They're not supposed to be smoking at all", ran through my mind. What I didn't know was the reality that was household routine was on the rise to crescendo.

Not long after that, Franco came on the scene. Beatriz walked in with him one evening, we were introduced and a day or two after that the student I'd heard about materialized. So there we were, a full house and I kept thinking about what the teacher'd told me, marveling at the uncanniness in the timing of events like they were prophecies. I had a fleeting thought if it all weren't being staged. But why? Interesting. Things were going to get even moreso. For the most part when Franco and Beatriz got together they stayed out for the weekend. I assumed she must stay at his place, thought again of the teacher and considered this situation wasn't turning out so bad - my mistake:

A Friday afternoon about a week later, Franco came over and got right down to pouring he and Beatriz a drink, he being whiskey, she being gin, so I guessed he'd planned to stick around. They both wanted to be social, ask me questions and talk about themselves. I'd gone into the kitchen to use the corkscrew and was hijacked for conversation on my way back to the bedroom. They learned I'd been divorced twice and I learned they were both separated, not divorced and had been seeing each other for a while. That's ok by me. This isn't uncommon in the U.S. and people have a right to their own lives as far as I'm concerned. We shared a drink, I put aside the wine I originally planned on having with my meal for a celebratory shot of whiskey, went back to my room to finish eating, then went out for one of my investigative journeys around Madrid. I loved walking around and making new discoveries – how roads connected, what restaurants were around, a new café, a new shop, grocery stores; maybe like those I used to frequent in Italy. When I returned Beatriz told me I could watch TV at night if I wanted to. It struck me as a result of our bonding moment I was moving up in the world and allowed the same privilege as the student. She also told me I should eat at the table in the living room. I wondered if I'd get to wash my own clothes soon.

After the breakthrough, or so I thought, Franco started to spend more and more time at the apartment. When I would come home in the evenings it'd seem like no one was there but then he'd burst out of Beatriz' room in a hurry to get her a sandwich before the bars all closed. Beatriz would just lounge in bed while she waited for him. Sometimes he'd pass me in the metro station, leaping and bounding down escalator stairs, the determined passionate lover on his mission. He'd notice my passing and shoot me a helpless, "you know she always asks for a sandwich at the worst time" look. I'd nod back an acknowledgement of his plight coupled with a kindly sardonic, "you poor guy" look while I couldn't help but wonder about their relationship. When I'd return home after my morning lessons, the two of them'd just be getting up walking around in their bathrobes. Smoking was confined to the bedroom although the smell was now stronger, which is what told me he was there. "Well, as long as they keep it in the bedroom". Nope, not going to happen.

Chapter 5: Loud Sex and Smokin' Cigarettes

Franco was around the house entirely too much, in fact, he slept over all the time and the evening sandwich run became a predictable ritual. Just in case it couldn't get any more interesting, it did. I can't honestly say if the moans and other sounds of obvious sexual activity came before or after the sandwich but thanks to my room being right next to Beatriz', I was sometimes wakened by them or had difficulty falling asleep because of them. You'd think they'd go to his place for the sake of privacy. (That teacher I'd met at the school had left a book behind, so when this occurred I'd read. After the fourth time, and it was a good book don't get me wrong, I made it a point to get to La Casa del Libro to buy a different one.) My patience with the whole situation was beginning to wear thin. Meanwhile:

I came home from teaching one afternoon and found the student in his room packing while Beatriz hovered and fawned. He was going home to visit his family then going to another city to continue university studies. I heard opportunity knocking and after he'd left told Beatriz I'd like to take his room. While I was praising my new potential living space and talking about what it had to offer, I didn't mention how the move would get me away from the sounds of the night's tète a tètes. Tranquility would be located between the kitchen and the bathroom. She agreed and I moved in. This room was bigger, had a better wardrobe and a large, empty dresser. There was a round bedside table with an antique chair and a lamp. The bed was bigger and had space beneath it to house my suitcases. I even chose the best of the best hangers from the closets in both rooms to hang clothes on. The spot was perfect. Beatriz and Franco could swing from the light fixtures in her bedroom and I wouldn't hear a thing. Peace would reign if but only for a short while:

Another afternoon and all afternoon I'd guesstimated, Franco and Beatriz had been drinking heavily. I'd come home from teaching and once again could smell smoke through the door before I entered the apartment, which did not make me happy. When I opened the door the living room was filled worse than when Beatriz and her friend were playing cards. Again, it must've been the overwhelmed and distressed look on my face that inspired them to jump up, not without difficulty, open windows and air out the place. As usual I'd gone to my room to toss my books on the bed and change. When I came out they were melodramatic and slurring apologies, so I decided I had to tell Beatriz, in case the school hadn't mentioned it – the only reason this could possibly be happening, that I'd asked for a non-smoker for the apartment-share and this was a bit too much for me. They cut me off before I could say any more, carried on about keeping the windows open, blowing the smoke out the windows, (which never works) and empty promises until the next time from now on, astonishingly similar enough to when someone does too much partying with drinking or drugs and feels the sudden emotional urgency to bargain with God to let them live. In spite of their heartfelt assurance I was becoming less and less happy about this whole deal. The place had become a real drag. When I wrote that I thought, "a drag of a cigarette", but I never intended a pun. Over the years, drag has evolved; not only does it mean boring, uninteresting, and not much fun but it also implies a place that gives off bad karma you want to get away from. I guess I could've said the situation was a bummer – and it was. Anyway, onward.

Just So You Don't Think It Was All The Same Drama:

A fellow teacher who I worked with invited me over for a get together with her newly acquired friends of the art district and other teachers. Mabel lived in Lavapies (pronounced lava-pee-ays), which means a place to wash your feet, that has become a section of town many immigrants live. Being an American determined to live in Madrid, possibly permanently, she (and her husband too if he wanted to hang out with his wife) found an apartment and settled there, and it happened to be part of one of the routes I frequently used when I lost myself to Madrid, that housed one of my favorite locutorios and a market that sold an excellent conditioner. Thanks to this get-together, Orlando, then a grad student who would soon become an assistant professor at his university, befriended me. One evening he invited me and another friend to accompany him to meet his boyfriend.

We sat for a while and for whatever reason the boyfriend didn't show, but we managed to have a nice time nonetheless. Orlando didn't seem to be all that surprised by the way things were turning out. Between 2 and 3 A.M. I threw in the towel and decided to head home. I was amazed at how busy the streets were in the evening (well, evening to me but the wee hours), not as busy as during the day but busy with the workers who took care of the city: sanitation, maintenance, street sweepers, whoever had a job for the purpose of upkeep. I walked home quickly being almost 2 hours away realizing a lot of people had my back.

The next day, as I thought about the evening before, I decided to compose (I'm using 'compose' loosely) an inane country, western spoof song about my friend being left stranded by his boyfriend:

Left in Lavapies

I was a sittin' on a bench
A bench nearby the street
Waitin' for my love
A love I know's so sweet

I waited and I waited
But no one ever came
In the middle of the night
I kept a wishin' his name

But he left me, he just left me
'Till early that A.M.
Just a sittin' and a wishin'
The morning my only friend

So, I walked home real slowly
Feelin' heavy and alone
Good thing I live close by
Close by and not far to roam
Left in Lavapies on a bench by the street
As the couples walked by me
Holding hands, cheek to cheek
Talkin' and a laughin'
While some just staggered drunk

But I was left in Lavapies
He left me there that skunk
I was left there on a street bench
How much that just stunk

Left in Lavapies,
*   left in Lavapies,*
*   left in Lavapies*
Relationship's all bunk

Left in Lavapies
*   left in Lavapies*
*   left in Lavapies*
Whiskey's gone, can't get drunk

Left in Lavapies
*   left in lavapies*
*   He left me, Lavapies*
Guess I could become a monk

Left in Lavapies
Left in Lavapies...

No worries; I'm not quitting my day job.

Chapter 6: Enter the Friend of the Family

Shortly after the "drunk-day afternoon" had come to pass, , a friend of Beatriz' daughter needed a place to stay in Madrid for the summer and came to live at the apartment. Simon occupied my old room and whether Beatriz liked it or not washed his own clothing. As soon as I noticed I asked him about it but he just shrugged and said Beatriz hadn't told him he couldn't. I saw another window of opportunity and followed suit. Like my showers I washed at obscure times which for the most part were when no one was around. It might sound silly but it felt great to separate my clothes into darks, lights and whites instead of watching in a mild terror that gripped my chest as Beatriz threw all of them into the wash together. Once she took laundry tablets packaged two together and tossed the unwrapped package into the machine with my clothes. I was dumbfounded which she brushed aside boasting she knew what she was doing. The package wasn't water soluable, the instructions were clearly stated in Spanish that even I understood; besides, commonsensically speaking, two tablets were too much detergent for the load. When I removed my clothes from the machine, all I was allowed to do, I checked to make sure all the soap had been rinsed out and salvaged what was left of the tablets. At any rate, washing my own clothes went well for a while but it wasn't going to last. Beatriz became aware of what we were doing. She didn't like it much but didn't say anything which I took as a positive sign that all mught just remain well thanks to Simon's presence; however,

One night I had put on a wash later than usual. Beatriz and Franco had gone out which usually meant they weren't coming back until sometime the next day, possibly the day after. I'd stayed up for a while watching TV but by the time the program was over the load still wasn't done. I was drowsy so I went to my room to lay down leaving the kitchen and my bedroom windows, cat-e-cornered to each other, opened to listen for when the machine finished. I dozed off and was awakened by the sound of Beatriz and Franco coming in. "Damn", I thought to myself but it was too late to do anything about it. They paused at the kitchen door, spoke with each other for a few minutes and went into her room. Franco came out, went into the kitchen and began clang-tinkering around. I knew my clothes were done but while I was waiting for him to leave, (I'd decided to "lay low" preferring no confrontation) I dozed off again. When I came to I heard the washer still going which was impossibile because I knew the cycle'd ended. I went into the kitchen and saw it'd been restarted. Why on earth would he do that? I let it wash again but now the machine wasn't working right. The spin cycle mysteriously wasn't functioning, the water wasn't draining so the clothes couldn't spin dry. I knew the outcome of clothes soaking in dirty rinse water for hours'd be a moldy smell that might never wash out. I was more stunned than angry even when it occurred to me that Beatriz may try to blame me for damages. A covert operation was in order. At whatever wee hour in the morning it was, I managed to get the washing machine door open and prop a bucket beneath it to catch the water as I took my clothes out and rinsed them by hand in the kitchen sink. When I was through, I made certain the door of the washer was closed and the dial set on cycle complete. Content, having decided my next course of action, I peacefully fell back to sleep in my bedroom decorated in hanging and draped garments.

Franco and Beatriz rose early that morning, something they never did, and walked directly to the washer in the kitchen. I was already up making toast, a very tasty culinary tradition with grated tomato and olive oil. I looked at the both of them in a joking, surprised, what-are-you-doing-up way, nodded toward the washer, shrugged and asked "what happened?" Beatriz went on about how she should be the only one to wash clothes and I just looked at them both with innocent blankness and said "I've never had a problem with it." She was insistent and so was I with my dumb innocence. I listened to her continue on, shrugged again and agreed, although I had no intention of ever letting her touch my clothes again, "OK, if that's what you really want", as if she'd never said anything about it in the first place. I also had no intention of staying there any longer. Laundry sabotage! What would be next! It'd all've been so much easier if the machine were a top loader.

I called the agency that'd originally sent me the photos of Beatriz' apartment, a "good opportunity" for me, and had a heartfelt conversation with the rental agent. She kept beating around the bush finally exclaiming Beatriz had sworn she'd quit smoking. I told her about all the things the teacher'd told me, the other events that'd taken place and expressed great dismay at being placed somewhere she already knew wasn't good only one week after the other teacher'd been moved out. I reminded her, which I thought the better approach would be to imply we all already know this, that Beatriz didn't like foreigners, was more interested in the money she made from them and besides that, I had another witness to her bad behavior, which kept her quiet and listening: For a two week period before the arrival of Simon, a young student, Maria, had rented my old room. A few days after she'd moved in, at the first chance we were alone, she expressed how uncomfortable Beatriz made her feel and how Franco'd been giving her orders about what she could and couldn't do at the apartment. She wasn't allowed to smoke inside, he said go outside, which completely amazed me. Nothing stopped Beatriz and Franco, would her smoking have made all that much of a difference? It tugged at my heart she was so young; she shouldn't be smoking anyway. Beatriz had no problems setting rules and giving orders so what was he doing, staking a claim as **the** significant-other-head-of-hoousehold? Maria told me as women she and I were the same. She could tell I'm a mom, not only a teacher who likes to travel and she although a serious student, like me, likes to have fun. I appreciated hearing the way she translated her thoughts that I was one of the good guys! Beatriz, and she said this in a half-whisper concerned she might offend me, acted more like she was a prostitute. I was impressed with her respectful manner and could empathize knowing too well how alarming Beatriz' behavior could be. After I mentioned this small detail to the agent, she admitted it was all true. I followed up with a call to the school to ensure I was going to be placed elsewhere and was stumped when I told the tale about the washer, they weren't supportive about my deposit. Their attitude was "oh, just let her have it if she makes an issue about it". Just let her have it? Hmmmm. There was an implication lost to them in translation! The whole conversation was curiously negative but I let it go. They'd lost a woman who worked in the office, the one American they had quit to attend college in the States, and hadn't found a replacement yet. I let that upstage my own dilemma and decided not to worry. All that was left to do now was wait for the agent to locate a new place for me to live.

When I first came to Madrid I was very interested in seeing the Flamenco, which the Spaniards refer to as the Ballet. I'd even hoped to take lessons and learn it for balancing, blueprinting, practical exercise but mostly fun. After living with a self-centered ex-flamenco dancer, I became as turned off by the thought of it as I was the bullfight. As time wore on after Beatriz, I'd see dancers around the city practicing in the streets (always on individual square boards), but was unmoved. I'd had my fill. As for the bullfight, it had nothing to do with living in Madrid. Growing up I'd seen them televised usually on a Sunday afternoon. I've always had a soft spot for the bull in question and prefer he not fight. If he has to, I'd rather the matador do no more than wave the red cloth gauntlet while attempting to dodge the bull's advances. If he remains lucky, he can leap over the bull a few times for entertainment symbolizing a victory dance calling it a day - olé! When all is said and done, the bull can be sent back to pasture to graze in the grass, protect his field, and reproduce little bulls and cows. I did eventually become a Madrileño, a resident of Madrid (protective of my city) who loses patience with tourists displaying poor manners and insensitivity toward the culture, but if there were a ballot box somewhere, I'd vote no bullfight.

While We Wait For The Agent To Call Back

This isn't exactly a chapter, it's just something to do while we wait:
I attended what turned out to be an all-nighter send-off bash for the American who was quitting. We, all of the school's teachers and the owners, met at a restaurant-club; restaurant upstairs, club downstairs, and around 2A.M. I decided to catch the metro and head home only to find out the trains stop running at 1 and don't run again until 6. I hadn't brought excess cash with me because I had a special travel pass for the metro/train and had thought I wasn't going to need any. Although I said I'd wait until 6, the teacher from Holland jumped to my aid and combed out our colleagues for contributions so I could take the bus. Before I stepped out to the bus stop a colleague put the moves on me to get me to go home with him, first

with a drink and then sexy suggestion. I can still feel his alcohol-soaked breath spray in my hair as he stumbled into my ear to whisper, "do you want to?" What I did do was point him in the direction of a woman who I knew wanted him. He was happy with that and once he was better situated I left to wait for the bus. Outside I had a great time watching the casino across the street: people were in and out, the police were in and out, and once or twice an ambulance pulled up. A group of college students staggering up the street stopped for directions and decided to practice their English, so I conducted a street side class for a few intoxicated youth of Madrid, (it was great - slurring is universal) and the bus I was supposed to take arrived but didn't want to let me off where I needed. It wasn't much longer until 6A.M., so I sat on a bench, continued watching the night life, appreciated that my friend from Holland had raised 20 euro for me, and reflected on, "I can say I was up all night at a club in Madrid".

Chapter 7: Away From the Famous Paseo and Toward the Town Center

Within reasonable time I got a call. "I think this is a good opportunity for you. Better than living with Beatriz. These two people are business partners. They own a store together. I sensed some good kharma when I spoke to them. There's definitely good kharma there. They smoke but not in the house. They take it outside so their flat doesn't get dirty from smoke." Knowing the agent was a South American living in Spain, I was impressed with her use of kharma while my teacher-brain mused if she really understood what it meant. I mentally gave her A-plus for effort and asked the same question I'd asked the first time, "is this for long term?" Most schools require a year's contract. The schools where I taught wanted me to stay for the calendar teaching year. "Yes, they want someone long term. They said definitely long term." She gave me the contact information for my second good opportunity and I arranged to meet one of my potential roommates (or flatmates if you're British), a woman named Mattia, the next evening.

Mattia was unique looking in her baggy hippie-era cotton clothing, earth sandals and Amelie haircut. As we spoke one of the first things she stressed was how much she and her associate both wanted someone to stay long-term. They were equally upset that the last person to live with them, a close friend of theirs, had left unexpectedly. She asked how long I intended to stay and I told her at least a year if not longer. She expressed the longer the better. I was ecstatic! Those were the words I'd wanted to hear. In fact, I was so ecstatic I forgot about the smoking, nevermind the alarm that should've gone off in my brain about the close friend. I'd need to get the keys from her partner which would also give him the chance to meet me before I moved in. She showed me the room and I left on a very high note. A night later I met Gonzalo, got keys and enjoyed a glass of vino tinto, red wine, as we talked. My new room was bigger, had a nice-sized closet with a rod that ran from side to side, a large dresser, wicker furniture, a desk - just great! I was told I could move in anytime and bring things over at my convenience. The location was toward the older part of town at a place where my peace would begin to return as I was out walking to get away from Beatriz and the antics going on, the town center. Not only that, but the metro was one and one half blocks away and one of the city's main train stations, Nuevos Ministerios, was only three long blocks down the street giving me easy access for travel in any direction. Good kharma most definitely along with an authentic good opportunity! I didn't realize how naive I still was.

Returning to my soon to be ex-apartment, I began packing and two evenings after my meeting with Gonzalo I brought a suitcase over. A couple of days later I brought another one. Over the weekend I finished moving and had my new place in Madrid organized. Being closer to the Town Center (known as Sol), meant I'd be exploring new routes to walk because I certainly wasn't going to shorten any of my journeys. I was set on getting to know Madrid. I anticipated new streets, new markets, shops and grocery stores. Being so close to the train meant I could return to Madrid after teaching out of town, stop in somewhere for a café con leche: espresso and a lot of steamed milk traditionally poured into a tall glass as opposed to a coffee cup for the purpose of burning your fingers when you try to pick it up as best I can figure, then walk back to the train station to head out for my next class. I was extremely happy with all the possibilities. What was most important was I finally had a place in Madrid, Spain. Now I could exhale.

Gonzalo and Mattia weren't going to turn out as dramatic with the potential for traumatizing as Beatriz, but they did have quirks and ultimately they'd turn on me.

Chapter 8: Mildly Disturbing Behavior

With the weekend off and not having to teach early Monday morning, I had time to go shopping to fill the spaces reserved for me in the refrigerator and kitchen cabinet. When I came home, Mattia was in the kitchen. She'd finished cooking for herself, had her plate and was about to go into the living - dining area to eat as I'd begun unpacking my groceries. As I put dinner napkins I'd bought on the top of the fridge, noticing she paused, put her plate down, put her napkin away, reached up, grabbed the package, opened it and took a napkin. After putting the package back, she gathered up her plate and utensils and went into the living room not saying one word to me. I was surprised she didn't ask but I didn't say anything. It's not uncommon for certain items such as napkins, paper towels, dish detergent and toilet paper to be used and replaced by all who share the house or apartment. It wasn't mentioned during our first meeting so I later spoke to Mattia offering money toward household goods but she was aloof brushing at the air with her hand. Huh? Most everything they used came from their store. If I wanted to use something different I'd have to buy it on my own. Ok, that's normal. Most of us have our favorite products but the topic of community sharing was glossed over and my offer flippantly dismissed. Ok, I felt I haven't even been here for five minutes yet but I'll keep an eye on things, mine in particular.

The paper towels I'd bought didn't hold the same attraction as the napkins did. I decided to use them as napkins in case the actual napkins ran out and weren't replaced. I felt kind of bad about what I considered a newly developed poor attitude up until I noticed eggs missing. Then other foods disappeared. I thought to myself, "my kids are grown, on their own; it takes time to get used to but it's nice to only take care of myself. I don't want to feed kids again." I learned to place things on top and in front of the egg carton and keep it toward the back of the refrigerator, out of sight, out of mind. There were traces of nationalism lingering in the air with Mattia and Gonzalo, both from a village near to the Basque region, so groceries

I bought at international chains that weren't Spanish went untouched. For the dry goods, keeping unopened packages of dry beans in front of whatever I had in the closet worked like a charm. I kept bottles of wine in my room but diplomatically offered them especially to Gonzalo who was more conscientious, and who insisted I use his laptop when he wasn't instead of spending money at the local locutorios for internet. I noticed my bread was safe if kept cool in the fridge. Day by day I learned what was in demand, what wasn't and how to protect what was.

A perk of the apartment offered as part of the rental agreement, inspiring me to look no further, was my own bath. There was no waiting, a bidet, a large tub and a huge toiletries cabinet but as the serpent slithered through paradise, I seemed to have one slithering around my bathroom. I noticed my shampoo and conditioner weren't lasting as long as they should (a little different than at Beatriz' - when I'd open my suitcase, which doubled as a supply cabinet, to get out toiletries I had cause to concern over "weren't there two – how many did I originally bring?") and on occasion too close to the last time, my bathroom was being used. Like I'd done for the kitchen I formulated a covert course of action. I had what I called backup toiletries along with good stuff. I started keeping good stuff in the back of the closet in my room and left backup toiletries in plain view along with what already had been used; once they ran out all that I'd leave would be the backups. The toilet paper went on top of the cabinet, out of the direct line of vision. At least the cleaners weren't used; I didn't buy them at their shop so the quality, as in what we sell is better than what you buy anywhere else, was in question. Fine with me. I take the good when it comes around and I began to partially close the door as a subtle hint.

I was happy with the location. Being able to begin walks from from a part of town that very much appealed to me was great. Having to be constantly aware of the whereabouts of my things was wearing.

Chapter 9: Beloved as a Flatmate or Roommate Depending on What Country You're From

I found out from a British colleague that flatmate and roommate hold two different meanings. For Americans, roommate simply means the person you share your apartment or dorm with so in American English, roommate would be equivalent to flatmate. For everyone else in the world, roommate means someone you share your bedroom with and implies something more intimate. So, if you go on a gameshow and are asked this question and win a bi-zillion dollars because you were the only one who knew the answer - you're welcome.

One of my goals with the move was to be able to retrieve some things I'd left in Italy at a friend's apartment. Now that I was in a situation that was long term, I planned a holiday to Italia. One of the good things about many European countries is the holy day, whether it be a saint's day or another noteable celebration they're always combined with the weekend making a surplus of days off. They have a knack for that balance of work and life plus practical thinking. After all, it would be senseless to have one day off by itself in the middle of the week. Where can you go, what can you do with so little time? When you are a contracted instructor, you get paid for all your holidays, like one to Italia! Even if you're an American without government permits or working papers, if you are fortunate enough to work for a school that gives you a contract anyway you've got it made. Part of my planning included continued reaffirmation of confirmation from Mattia and Gonzalo they did indeed want me to live at the apartment for an extended period of time. "Yes of course" they both reassured me. "We love having you here." Right up until I left I'd bring it up to make certain for certain I could live there two years if I wanted. The answer was always yes, yes, yes, semper fideles yes! Off I went confident and secure. When I returned I happily unpacked and rearranged my room to accommodate things I hadn't seen in over a year, however; there were a couple of changes that had taken place in my absence I had to deal with:

Mattia had a cleaning fit for herself and decided to discard a container of mine I used for food storage. Seemed minimal but I'd brought three with me that were the perfect size for my intents and purposes and kept them, at her behest, with the other house containers. I'd brought back food I wanted to repack and store. "Oh well" I thought to myself as I came up with a creative way to keep the other two in my room for safe keeping when I wasn't using them. Later on I mentioned something to Mattia about my loss. "I knew it wasn't mine or Gonzalo's but I didn't want that shape in the cabinet anymore. I wanted to use just the square ones." I forgave her but asked she give them back next time and I'd keep them out of her way. The other was that my bathroom had obviously been used. Gonzalo was home when I noticed so I shot him a raised-eyebrows peaceful-frown look, placed some things back in the cabinet and gently but firmly clicked the door shut. This was as safe as the bathroom was going to be from intruders. I felt using my bathroom without permission was the same as walking into my room when I had the door closed. It's better diplomacy to ask and I wasn't subletting.

A week or two after my return smoking inside, as opposed to outside so no smoke residue gets on the walls, became popular. The living-dining area was now the smoking room and if I wanted to watch television at night I'd have to endure it. Mattia'd break out her dad's home made sherry, share it with everyone else but me when we were in the same room together. She held get-togethers that were closed to me. According to her, my Spanish wasn't good enough to warrant hanging out with their friends. Rather than go about their business and do what they'd normally do as friends with friends, I didn't expect to be invited to things just because I happened to live there, it was necessary I know I wasn't invited. It struck me as odd and for a fleeting moment got caught in wondering why but I stopped that in its tracks and wasn't going to dwell on it. As for my Spanish, although both of them are part of a culture that normally enjoys intercambio, the exchange of languages, they weren't generous when it came to conversation.

Intercambio is very popular at many pubs and select clubs around Madrid. Businesses select a slow night out of the week for holding an intercambio and advertise in local newspapers. The event details are posted on a chalkboard for listing offertas, daily specials, and set out on the sidewalk. Who wouldn't want to meet that intriguing stranger who speaks another language, especially much-in-demand English? It usually begins around nine p.m. and is very good for luring international clientele. Mattia and Gonzalo constantly pressed me for free English lessons and I'd gladly comply but when it came time for the exchange the interest in speaking ended. Gonzalo, who was forever telling me "I know you are a good teacher, you speak very slowly and clearly", was more interested in practicing than Mattia. I would joke about it in a positive way but in all seriousness wished they spoke Spanish to me more often. Gonzalo'd laugh out loud at the suggestion, fire something at me in Spanish and then walk away not giving me a chance to respond. Spanish is spoken very rapidly, so when Gonzalo fired Spanish at me he was talking faster than any New Yorker could - a point I used to stir up students "do you know you talk faster than I do!" Hearing that gave them the courage to keep practicing. Nonetheless, I tried to take advantage when he pressed me for lessons to get a few grammar tips. Mattia considered herself fluent in English and would interfere by interpreting for Gonzalo. This wasn't good - she wouldn't accept she could be wrong. Sadly familiar with one-way street relationships, I could see what was going on around me was turning into just that. I could live with it if I had to. It wasn't necessary we all become bosom buddies but again it tugged at my heart-strings that coexisting wasn't going to be happier. Couldn't we fall into a routine, leaving a door open for experiencing tolerance? I never expected the outcome.

By now my napkins had run out and the ones that were there first were back in use. I kept up with my paper towels and things stabilized for a while. I wasn't all that interested in watching TV at night anyway after a long day of traveling and teaching and Gonzalo at least closed the living room doors to confine the smoke.

I was as pleasant as humanly possible when I used the kitchen, offering supplies when either of them were out of something. Gonzalo got to the point that he replaced things he used so we developed a better rapport. Mattia was trying to hold what she believed to be her ground as dominating matron of the house. With all due respect that didn't exist toward me at all, I am a good twelve years older than she. I'd earned the position long before we'd met but I was more interested in harmony. So it goes and so stability went as well.

Although Gonzalo continued to close the livingroom doors when he smoked and open the windows to air it out when he was going to bed, smoking in the house kept getting worse. He also smoked in his room, often left the bedroom door open instead of closing it like he'd been in the habit of doing and at the same time became careless about what he wasn't wearing when he walked around. One had to stop and marvel "what on earth is going on now!" His girlfriend slept over a lot; she's a lovely person who never minded bantering Spanish with me. For reasons unknown Gonzalo made more and more of a habit of walking around in his underwear which I didn't appreciate; he would stand in his doorway in full view clad only in briefs. When I'd notice him, he'd give me that look that I'd seen before: the knowledgable acknowledgment of "yes, I'm desirable". Honestly, no he wasn't but in any case there weren't any inciting sparks: I saw what he was doing as thoughtlessness toward his girlfriend and generally speaking, I just don't consider this form of foreplay a good way to promote a solid relationship or friendship. What I didn't suspect and what I discovered later on was I was being baited for a reaction. I wasn't considering any of his actions seriously enough. What was on my mind was Madrid had become my life, I worked for three very good schools and had obligations to them. I was happily otherwise occupied.

Chapter 10: Going and Gone

Mattia decided to go to England and brush up on her command of English. I helped her format a resumé, called a CV in Europe, so she could work at a small market near to where she wanted to stay. When her plans were finalized she told us she'd be gone for three months. I was immensely relieved, restraining myself from turning cartwheels down the hall (they would've been my first) and thought at this time in this place, life couldn't get much better. Not long after she left that emotion and my miserably wrongful attitude were going to cost me again. Oblivious to my fate, I discussed with both Mattia and Gonzalo we should have a send-off dinner and I encouraged Mattia she'd speak with a British accent by the time she returned. "Yes. Dinner's a great idea!" Time ticked by and I kept reminding Gonzalo more than Mattia, seeing she was frequently out celebrating her bon voyage with friends, about the dinner. "No problem! We'll do something!" The last time I saw Gonzalo to remind him, he was off to stay with her at their village to celebrate her departure. She'd be back very late to pack and then leave very early. Hmmmmph. At least the tension that was always present would be gone. During packing, one of the throw pillows from my bed became gone too. After her departure, Gonzalo started throwing luncheons I was always invited to. He and his girlfriend went away more often leaving me with his laptop. I saw his actions as a release, similar to mine, from Mattia's dominance. I kept thinking about what I thought was the reality that I had a place, Mattia notwithstanding, in Madrid. I knew she'd be in a better frame of mind when she returned but in all honesty, I didn't have it in me to look forward to it. There was an overcast twinge of dread in the air but I was determined to enjoy the time I had.

I was up early one morning to immerse myself in the peacefulness that is the city before it awakens with a café con leche in a coffee cup (there wasn't a Madrileño in sight to tsk-tsk my choice and Gonzalo didn't care). I sat in the kitchen with the door closed so not to disturb him in case I tinkered around. After an endless amount of time, I heard signs of life from down the hall. He staggered into the kitchen and sat across from me. We exchanged good mornings, buenas dias, and then he said he wasn't certain how to say what he wanted to tell me. I didn't think what was going to be said would amount to anything more than another free English lesson. I sat up straight, focused, folded my hands in my lap and said "Don't worry. Take your time." What I first understood was that the owner of the apartment was coming back and I was in his room so I'd have to give it up. He was going to decide if he wanted to live in Madrid permanently and if so I'd be without a place to stay. I was stunned. This was really bad timing. What this meant was my roommates weren't the proprietors they'd led me to believe they were, I wasn't one-third equal partner of the apartment, and they were subletting which is illegal in Madrid. Gonzalo took advantage of my state of shock to wax philosophical about the twists and turns of life. I rallied from my confusion to press on in order to find out why this was happening. Things were finally made clear. There was no owner of the apartment. Mattia and Gonzalo rented the apartment from the company that owned the building. Most of the people who lived in the building owned their apartments. I should've been put on the lease. What was going to take place was that a distant friend of Mattia's who happened to be from the village and who, as Gonzalo spun the yarn, she hardly knew at all, wanted to live in Madrid at our apartment. Gonzalo wanted him to have my room and wanted me to take Mattia's room. When he made his request, he looked at me with the same expression he'd given me when he stood in his bedroom doorway in his underwear. He then said, imploringly, he de-si-rrred I change rooms. An emotion surged within but I can tell you it wasn't what Gonzalo was fishing for. Desired! I had no intention of going along with any of this. When I thought it was the owner of the apartment I'd have no choice but to cooperate - not now. I could predict how things'd work out if I gave up my room especially should Mattia come back earlier than expected. For how long would I be moved into the living room before I'd be moved outside? Was *she* looking for a roommate (was that her *desire*)? At this stage my mind couldn't wrap itself around much else than I had to move again. I managed to stammer something about it's best I be out before I left for vacation.

I gave the rental agency that had set up my good kharma opportunity a call and I was not happy. What happened to long term? Why were my roomates allowed to break their contract with me? What protection did I actually get? Now I had a lot more things to be concerned with. Long term availability had been confirmed and based on that I'd brought back things from Italy so there were more personal effects to cart around. I also had a non-refundable plane ticket for a vacation to see my daughter and the rest of my family over the holidays. I told the woman in the office I wanted to be moved out before my departure date, plus I'd follow-up with an email to confirm the request and remind her to reaffirm what we discussed and decisions made with Gonzalo. After all, I was paying her wasn't I? Why was I paying her? What was I paying her for exactly? It kept nagging at me that I wasn't better protected than this. She argued there was nothing she could do if those providing housing changed their minds mid-stream. I was flabbergasted. I inquired about my contract. I had guarentees, didn't I? She told me it had nothing to do with who I lived with. The proprietors had a separate contract with open ended rules. Mine was for housing only, she'd been finding me housing and when it doesn't work out I get moved. My mind went momentarily blank. OK. Why sell me long term when there's no such thing? I was beside myself with the realization I had no protection at all and I was paying for it. Was this some kind of joke? The agent ranted about the good job she's been doing for me and how hard she works. This is what she meant by "taking care of things" and "nothing (for me) to worry about". According to these terms, once you're moved it makes no sense to unpack. I asked at that point what exactly her commission was for. I was told she didn't get to keep the commission but had to give it to the school as a fee for being allowed to rent apartments for them. She makes no money and the school makes all the money. It wouldn't be long after this happened that one of the owners of the school would tell me they didn't make money on the rentals. The rental agent gets all the fees and deposits. I couldn't help but wonder how business survives. Odd place Spain is. At any rate, with questions answered unsatisifactorily, things were left at being resettled somewhere before I left for vacation. I wasn't feeling very confident with the turn of events and the lack of support from both sides of the fence. The agent became arrogance I hadn't experienced before and the school was cold about all that was going on. Since the American left their office I'd felt the American teachers'd lost their advocate voice, but at the same time, lurking was the realization she hadn't been honest with me in her presentation of the school, nor of the requirements of the Spanish govenment (as I was learning) both of which took away from the marketed benefit of teaching in Madrid. I can appreciate life experience but it was unnerving as things kept unravelling, narrowing down and pointing at something that was no more than a money-making scheme. Not much further down the road I'd confirm the true nature of what I had gotten myself into: the reality of Spanish adventure.

Chapter 11: Radio Silence

I kept busy working as I very much looked forward to my holiday. The only reason I looked forward to moving was the peace I'd have being re-settled somewhere else safe and sound. Oddly, or shouldn't I have been surprised, the rental agent became distant. I emailed to no avail. After almost a month I recieved a response about a good opportunity way above what I was used to paying. I knew other teachers were getting moved into nice less expensive places. I let her in on this fact. My requirements hadn't changed so there shouldn't be any problems. Communication went silent again. I contacted another agency hoping between the two I'd stand a better chance. I was relieved they were interested in helping me and went to the office to brainstorm about areas that'd accommodate my travel needs. There was a room available in a location I particularly liked, so I took the information and made an appointment. The owner was a single business woman and the apartment was very nice. When we were considering finalizing everything she told me she was adopting a little girl so my stay'd be limited. It could be two months, five months, most likely no more than eight months before the child would arrive and the room she was renting me would be her room. I was disappointed and knew I couldn't risk the little girl arriving while I was away. Then what? I reported this to the agency who told of another place they'd let me know about as soon as it became available which should be in time before I left. I waited.

Communication went dead again and it was getting uncomfortably close to departure time. While all this was going on, Gonzalo cheerfully told me one evening Mattia was coming back around the time I was leaving, go figure, intended to stay at the apartment a few days and then head out to the village to stay with her father for a month. Well, what I certainly needed was added pressure to be out before she arrived. I knew, with me nowhere nearby to protect my stuff, she was going to help herself. By the time I returned she'd be gone. I had to be officially out before she came back permanently in January. I could find her, hopefully get back what she took but it shouldn't've had to've been a concern at all. I reminded Gonzalo about my moving out before December eighteenth. His responses ranged from "Don't worry, Mattia can stay in the living room one or two days" to "No Mattia's not coming at all. She's going to see her father straight from England." The second comment came after he'd spoken to the rental agent when I'd called her a second time to reverify the conditions of Mattia's early return. I said to him, "Gonzalo, you told me Mattia was stopping at the apartment first." He smiled and said "Don't worry. Be happy." Everything was mounting up a little too much. I still hadn't heard back from my agent about new accommodation when the other agency finally contacted me about the apartment they'd told me about. I could go see it right away but the price had gone up a couple of hundred euro. I questioned the increase. "Well, it is in a very good location. A lot of people want to live there." I was extremely annoyed and stressed. I had to move, this was no joke and I wasn't about to put myself into a high financial risk situation.

I contacted the school and told them about everything. One of the owners got back to me saying neither agency wanted to help because my demands were too high. Only one of them could get away with that. I had a contract with the other and she was obligated, at the very least, to relocate me. The owner said my agent'd told her personally she didn't think she could accommodate me. This was nonsense. My requirements hadn't changed since I'd been there. What suddenly made my situation so unique? She also told me that my emails *demanding* different places to stay had compromised things. My emails were about different locations I could live, nothing too tough to understand, widening the spectrum of possibilities to make the agent's job easier. Had kharma and fluency stepped out? By the agent's refusal to move me our contract was broken. I should've recived my deposit back plus fees then and there. My stress level reached new heights I can tell you. I began searching adds in the paper for apartment shares realizing I wouldn't be able to depend on either agency. The owner then recommended a couple of places. I called one who did a poor job of stiffling an outburst laugh when I told him my name saying he'd already rented the room. I called another who never returned my call. I reported this back and the owner remarked about how everyone wanted to know what a woman of my age was doing hanging around Madrid. Why wasn't I twenty-one and leaving after three months? First of all, who comprises "everyone"; second, what does my age have to do with anything? Hadn't they ever heard of ageless? The math is basic: I'm a teacher, I'm teaching. That's what I do and that was a strange remark to make in any case. What happened to the testimony about being able to live in Madrid for at least a year? Did she completely forget a big part of why I was there was because of that perk alone? Did she forget the American who'd worked in the office sold me on the fact she'd lived there two years herself without worry? I didn't think the owner'd be getting any prizes for business diplomacy after that. At least I wouldn't have awarded her anything. She asked me again when I needed to be out by, what was ideal for me. I reminded her and she came up with another recommendation: a friend who lived on the outskirts of Madrid in a residential area. I took the information and contacted Lorine.

Lorine is a British South-African, around my age, a teacher and another of the school's alumni. (Are you asking yourself what a woman of her age is doing hanging around Madrid?) She'd been living in Madrid a little over a year. As we sat at the apartment sipping wine and discussing me as a potential roommate, I asked if she required a deposit. I'd hoped to wait until money was refunded from the agency. She said not to worry, then showed me around. The room she'd selected for me had more than ample closet and drawer space. There were three bedrooms but the one in the middle of hers and mine she suggested we use as an office or anything we wanted. There was a roomy kitchen, a bathroom with a space-age shower stall (it had massage jets with four control knobs - one wrong turn and you might find yourself pasted to the stall door), and an alcove with a washer. My finalized rent was less than I'd been paying. I decided to take it and was given the option of moving in at my convenience. My rountine became work, packing and transporting. With a little help from Lorine the last day of packing, I managed to finish moving in three days before my departure to the States. Peace at last.

When the owner played such a strong hand in assisting me, I foolishly thought I'd finally been accepted into the fold that made up the school "family" and luck had put its arm around my shoulders. I wasn't actual alumni because I hadn't taken their course but I wasn't the first person they'd acted as agent for with jobs and housing. Part of that sales pitch was promoting that anyone doing business with them at any level comprised a part of their academy family. It'd been a grueling seven months. I stopped giving thought to what'd been said about why I was in Madrid; however, all wasn't going to be quiet on the front just yet. The business partner who'd eventually taken the American's place trumped the hand the owner'd played:

I met with the agent who was refusing to refund my deposit. She claimed she had no idea who the owner of the school was, therefore she'd never told her she'd refused to help me. By finding another place on my own I'd broken the contract which entitled her to keep the deposit. Gonzalo, she reported, was upset he didn't know I was leaving, the week I moved he'd been skiing in the mountains, and demanded an extra week's rent be covered. I was flabbergasted again. So she hadn't done her job even though there'd been open communication about moving me before the eighteenth. The distant friend from the village had moved into the apartment by then and taken over Mattia's room. When I'd taken the last of my things I let him know I was moved out; Gonzalo wanted him to have my room so when Mattia came back she could have her own room. He had been very surprised by all this news and why now made sense to me. I demanded to contact the school right there from the office. The new associate, Regina, answered the phone. I explained that the agent had agreed to refund me when I returned the keys and now that they'd been returned, she was refusing. Regina claimed they couldn't force her to pay me. I informed her that part of it had already gone toward one week's rent and only half the original amount was owed. Regina blurted "well, if that's all it is then pay it!" I reclarified that the amount was owed to me and she instantly reverted back to "we can't make her pay you." If I wasn't so emotionally worn and thinking a little more clearly I could've turned to the agent and said "she said if that's all there is you should just pay it". That might've confused the issue enough to get the cash back but I was too stumped and in a state of momentary-overwhelmed-awestruck, from witnessing the reality of fascist era behavior techniques I'd studied about in film classes when I was a university undergraduate. I was in the middle of it and couldn't believe what I was hearing. Nonetheless, this all was rediculous. Continuing on, I demanded clarification of the agent not knowing nor speaking with the owner . Regina asked to speak with her. As soon as the agent got on the phone she began their conversation by apologizing for my bad behavior, she had no idea what I was talking about, I was just talking crazy and then asked, "who is this Nancy anyway, I've never met her" not even trying to suppress her grin. My throat caught and I held back tears. I'll be damned! There was no denying what was taking place now. I received some sarcastic ridicule from Regina when I got back on the phone because of the shakiness in my voice, "oh sure – you just go and enjoy your holiday – awwwww... awwwww"; I let it go. It was finished for now but I wasn't finished with it yet. There was too much good going on otherwise to let what was happening get me down. I had no worries about Lorine and I was going to see my daughter and the rest of my family soon. I was bringing goodies from Madrid for everyone and I'd be bringing back some items to add to what I already had. In spite of it all, bits of my life were coming together.

In the States I had a wonderful time. On my return my new roommate had a surprise waiting. She'd had a New Year's Eve party and saved a bottle of champagne and plastic flutes that contained twelve white grapes. The grapes signified a year of good luck. We ate grapes, drank and conversed about anything that came to mind. I'd brought back books, CDs, sewing notions, small baskets, along with supplies that cost me a lot less than they do in Europe. I now had very little left my daughter was holding for me. With all I'd been through, I still believed I'd be able to live in Madrid indefinitely. I honestly thought my career was there. I had plans for my kids, times we'd spend together and places we'd see. I was planning when I'd visit my family. The possibilities were tremendous. The following day I very happily unpacked and organized my new room. The third time was not going to be the charm.

Chapter 12: My Ex In Drag

Things moved along smoothly. Besides the apartment being perfect and the area absolutely idyllic, the walk to the metro that brought me into the city in two stops was a short one. I began to map out routes now around the suburbs and saw houses instead of only apartments. The train station was quite a distance from where I lived so finding it made for enjoyable exploration and on the way I found a shopping center plus a couple of inviting restaurants. The fact that I couldn't catch the train easily from where I was didn't present a problem. The second metro stop was Chamartin, another main station I could pick up the train. If I hadn't a gun to my head I'd never have considered living outside the city. I could've been in the fresh air sooner. During the first weeks I discovered Lorine had differences with Nancy, was angry about them and didn't like Regina at all. As the story unfolded: Nancy had stuck her nose into something she shouldn't have and cost Lorine work that kept her struggling for a good part of her first year in Madrid. Since she'd landed the job she had, finances were on the upswing. Needless to say she had severed all ties with the school. Puzzling. I'd been told Lorine was Nancy's friend. "Not after what she did."

Now that I was resituated and somewhat resuscitated, I wanted to delve back into the agent's claim of not knowing Nancy and Regina's complete absence of support. Curiously, those two things could never be cleared up by admission or denial. In fact, on showing up at the school and speaking directly to Nancy and her business partner, all I got as a response was Nancy's red face and the partner telling me they couldn't force the agent to pay me. It was then I was told how they don't make any money on the rentals, the agent does. It's completely out of their hands but because other of their students were also complaining, they were going to have a meeting with her. My complaint was top priority. I let it go again but wasn't going to forget about it. Meanwhile, another friend called offering a room. His last roommate'd moved out and he'd love to have me there. I'd have loved to've lived there but I felt I shouldn't move out so suddenly. Lorine seemed an awful nice lady and I had the impression she could use the money. As I reflect back on the events that followed mounting one after another like a volcano pushing up from the ground, I've come to realize I have to stop this habit of backing the wrong horse.

Very shortly after my friend'd called and made his offer, with just enough of a time lapse so I couldn't go back and take him up on it, Lorine's behavior began to change. Two patterns were developing. The least of my worries were the household complaints. On more than one occasion I came home to all the lights except my room turned on, along with both TVs turned on, her laptop left on while Lorine was talking on the house phone in our office with her cellphone in her hand in case she got a call. Although my utilities agreement had been finalized at a set rate, I vowed under my breath I wouldn't give one red cent more. Her bedroom TV went out unexpectedly, at least that was one less thing on, and it was required I give up watching time to be accommodating. When I would get home early enough there was an hour show I'd try to catch but it was reruns and not life and death that I see it. Lorine went on cleaning binges at night while I was trying to sleep. Her reason was she saw things she wanted cleaned, swept or vacuumed and was annoyed I didn't just do it when she thought I should. During my mid-day break I'd come home, eat, clean up after myself and do some minor straightening. Otherwise, my time for housework would be on the weekend thanks to my work schedule. As an American I had to work without a contract because I had no work permit. I'd been told that because the paperwork was a slow and tedious process, the government didn't care if American teachers didn't have any. The drawback was that without both work permit and contract, there were no benefits. Because of this, I took anything that was thrown at me. I thought it best to keep smiling and make myself most valuable player through cooperation, diplomacy and professionalism. My schedule became one of extremes. I rose early to travel to the four corners of Madrid to accommodate business professionals before their work day began and then traveled for evening classes when the work day ended. After getting home between ten and eleven o'clock at night with having to get up at six or seven the following morning, the last thing I wanted to do was mop the floor. Believe me, I've never had a problem with doing my share of housework. Usually I am taken advantage of because of my teamwork attitude. I knew having to remind her of this was a bad sign. I could feel it. Lorine went on laundry binges that occupied the washer and clotheshorse (for hanging and drying laundry) for up to two weeks. I would sometimes do a wash when she was mid-binge but not home and hang things around my room or I'd catch time between binges, which could be as short as a couple of days. On rare occasions I'd actually get to use the clotheshorse. Little things began cropping up like I didn't fold kitchen towels or hang them the way she wanted me to. Gradually my room became my domain. Too bad I had to appear to cook or take a shower. Now for what would become the worst of my troubles:

The other behavior pattern that was developing was oddly familiar to me from Skilled Nursing and Adult Psych Unit medical days... and somewhere else. But, where? In fact it wasn't long before Lorine's behavior began to read like a textbook. And then, to my dismay, it hit me that the chapters were about the alcoholic. Although I'd come across patients on the unit suffering from this time to time, the last alcoholic I had to seriously deal with I'd been married to: my second ex-husband. Just terrific. My ex in drag. I gruesomely mused about his dropping dead in a rehab and coming back as Lorine. I am told things happen for a reason. I wonder what this one was. Compounded experience and medical training snapped-to as I began to watch her behavior closely but discreetly.

At first I hadn't paid attention to how much she drank. During one of our first converstions, one that is almost everyone's first revelation when they come to Europe, that good quality wine is conveniently inexpensive, she quipped she thought she might be drinking too much. I quipped back that wine is good for your blood. We laughed together and the conversation carried on. She loved Spanish red wines and I noticed she was polishing off a bottle every other day. From what I'd seen of her drinking I'd categorize her as a lightweight - a few sips and she's slurring, a glassful makes her tipsy, half a bottle a day was way too much.

Gradually things began to escalate and coincide with what were the least of my worries. The more she drank, the more combative: argumentative, complaining and confrontational she became. First tier were the cutting remarks based on past conversations. She'd snap at me about anything, then stomp away. Second she took particular relish in revealing my imperfections to me but the greatest thing she said was I wasn't normal. When it happened she was to her brim with vino bravado. She cut me off as I was walking down the hall toward the bathroom and carefully slurred "There's something wrong with you. You're not normal. I'm normal but you're just different. Something's wrong and it's with you." I hadn't heard that since I was a child arguing with my cousins or school friends, "Nah-uh! My family's normaler than your family is". As amusing as the memory was it fell short of taking my mind off what was going on around me, besides the fact that she wanted me to fight with her about it. She looked at me with complete disgust and goaded, "you're not going to argue with me, are you?" She wanted physical confrontation. I found myself having to reconsider things I hadn't had to think about in years. I knew I couldn't continue living there with the situation so volatile and unsafe. I locked my bedroom door at night. When she wasn't avoiding me with complete disdain toward my presence, she was confronting me just because I was there.

Chapter 13: Peas With No Pods

As I was thinking about this next turn of events, part of a song from a favorite musical of mine kept running through my head: "two lost ships on the ocean of life, one with no sail and one with no rudder, but ain't it just great, ain't it just grand, we got each udder..." (actually, I just watched it a day or two ago and those aren't the lyrics exactly... but you get the picture). During the turbulence that took place thanks to my next move, I kept wondering " is this what a friend would have done? Did he do me a *favor*?"

I shared Lorine's problem with a good friend of hers, also a colleague of mine, whom I thought could help with the situation. I sent him an email about everything that had been going on and encouraged him that he and her other friends, closer to her than I was, could do wonders in aiding her to stop drinking. I've seen severe conditions and she wasn't that far gone yet. I mentioned that although I liked the apartment very much, I was looking for another place to stay. My reason for leaving could simply be the location was a bit too far out. There was no need to add fuel to the fire. I kept an eye on my email thinking he'd respond. A week passed by - nothing. There was no real reason to worry about his lack of response and my mind already had plenty on it. Life goes on - or not.

He'd decided to show her the email. When she came home after visiting with him one afternoon she exploded at me in the reveal-all of what she'd read. She interjected accusations of things I hadn't said but I wasn't allowed a response. The best thing to do was remain calm. During my medical days colleagues always appreciated the calming effect I had with patients, which in turn calmed them. I hoped I could keep that atmosphere going to come up with a solution.
 Lorine seized on the moment for further argument but I wasn't reacting according to how she wnted me to so she gave me an ultimatum to get out in one week. I didn't think it was possible but she didn't care if I had to live outside. I responded in soft, low tones keeping my expression serene. I managed to calm her down and buy myself a little more time but before the week was out she confronted me again about when I would be leaving. I gave her an update but that wasn't satisfactory so she gave me another ultimatum: pay her

the rent in advance or she was going to have me deported. When this'd begun I'd contacted my son, preparing him in case I might have to leave Madrid in a hurry and show up at his door. It was cheaper to get a plane ticket to him in Istanbul than it was to get one to the States on short notice. He'd been checking into things for me to verify what exactly I had in the name of rights in this situation. He let me know if she did call the police, she'd also cause a problem for herself simply because she's a fellow foreigner. I'd recently learned I wasn't supposed to be without working papers and contracts; it'd all come to light when three of the school's alumni were arrested and deported. The government does require American teachers to have both. The school held a special meeting following the incident and told alumni and new students alike to say they were tourists if questioned, not teachers. That meant if you remained longer than three months you were illegal. Drawing this kind of attention to me would definitely cause a problem but nonetheless she'd also be deported compliments of causing the trouble. The likelihood of her following through with her threat wasn't strong but I didn't want to chance it being way too familiar with the unpredictability of this type of behavior. Being a woman myself, I know how women can get. I got her to agree to take one week's rent and sent an sms to the friend who had offered me the room. I could've kicked myself for not taking him up on it. "Lorine threatened me. Is there anyone with closet space I can move into temporarily?" He called back instantly and asked what she'd said. When I told him he said I was to stay at his place. "But isn't your house full?" "Don't worry. You can have my room and I'll go stay with my boyfriend. He'll like that. I'm gone a lot on the weekend anyway. Maggie, we have to get you out of there."

Chapter 14: Enter Stage Gay

I could not thank Orlando enough. I had a lot to sort through between what I'd brought back from Italy and the States and what I already had with me. Still hopeful of somehow having a permanent home, I borrowed two big suitcases and began packing. What I decided I wouldn't keep I left neatly folded by the dumpsters in plastic bags, handled paper bags and an old carry-on. I'd gotten to know the refugees of the area and when they'd be by the dumpsters to see what'd been put out. Most of the community did the same. We neatly draped clothes and set other items on the closed lids and at the sides on the ground carefully packaged. There was one dumpster in particular that never had trash in it. Instead, it housed bags of useful things. Orlando stopped by within a couple of days to help cart suitcases to his place and set up a contingent plan to pick up the rest. A day or two later, I brought another two suitcases over on my own. My soon to be ex-roommate had no idea of what was taking place. With all that'd happened, I knew the best thing was to discreetly be gone. As my room emptied I began to feel better. New life awaited me and it was strengthening knowing I had a real friend in Madrid.

By Friday of that week I was completely packed. Orlando told me he was bringing an ex-boyfriend of his to help. While I sat in the living room watching TV, "Walker, Texas Ranger", Lorine came home and grunted in disgust when she saw me. I felt a sad heaviness in my chest, "Of all days, why did she have to come home early today?" Luckily she put music on and occupied herself in the kitchen. I got up and walked across the living room to look out the window and spotted Orlando walking and his friend Alvaro, sporting a single crutch, hobbling down the street. I was delighted and relieved as I thought "what is he going to carry... he could keep her at bay if she comes at us." When they entered, Orlando didn't like what he sensed.
"Your flat mate's home?" "Yeah, she's cooking." "I don't like the way it feels in here at all", Alvaro interjected as they exchanged glances of alarm. Orlando agreed and said "we'll take everything now. I don't want you to have to come back and get anything else." We pulled everything into the hallway, down the steps and out. Once

we were outside on the sidewalk Alvaro said "I'm Orlando's ex." I told him I already knew that as we exchanged traditional kisses on both cheeks. I gave Orlando a big squeeze-hug. Then, as good as any comedy team, we walked, hobbled, took turns with different-sized luggage and my standing fan that was too big to pack was tossed from shoulder to shoulder. I'd kept the key to the apartment; although Orlando didn't think I should, in case I'd forgotten something but I knew I hadn't. I returned it Sunday morning after I'd sorted through everything, given to Orlando what I wanted him to have and unpacked the things I was going to keep out for use. As I rounded the corner and was in sight of the apartment, I felt as if I were being watched. Did she expect I'd come in and try to say goodbye? Maybe she had officials there and we were all getting deported. Didn't matter. I didn't enter the apartment but dropped the key in the mailbox in the entryway. With no confrontation and no words exchanged, as I rounded the corner that rendered the apartment out of sight, I walked back to the metro feeling free.

Chapter 15: Where to Now? (Any Saint Who Hasn't Been Kicked Off the Calendar Yet, Hear My Prayer.)

Orlando's apartment was in my favorite area, Sol, the town center. I was one block from the Atocha station that all train lines pull into along with metro Line 1 which solved all of my traveling needs. He had a laptop and gave me his login and password so I had free internet and his roommates were terrific people! They were very interested in practicing their English and saw the value of my speaking Spanish well when speaking English got too complicated for them. I'd died and temporarily gone to heaven. Orlando told me not to worry about finding a place, relax, spend up to a month if I needed to and we'd look after that. I was safe. "Don't worry, be happy" ran through my mind. I smiled.

After a couple of weeks had passed, Orlando sent an sms about an apartment listing that'd just been posted at his university. I took the info to check it out. It was so nice not to have high stress about moving. I contacted one of the potential apartment-share mates and set up a time to come and see the room. The apartment itself was a spacious three bedroom with a livingroom, kitchen and balcony. Two students lived there and one'd just moved out. I was told there were a couple other people interested so they'd let me know who they chose. The room was particularly appealing to me because of it's layout. There were two desks: one computer desk and one Davenport, each with a chair. The closet was big and roomy with a built in dresser. There were two small end tables with drawer space. I kept my fingers crossed.

After about a week to a week and a half I was contacted as the prizewinner. I had to meet with the realtor, a woman who worked for the company that owned the building to sign a lease. We met at a café around the corner from the apartment, talked business and I signed. The two students, now flatmates, returned to the apartment with me and I paid the one who was designated bookkeeper rent and deposit.

It was extraordinarily cheap, about two-thirds of my last amount and I can tell you the timing was perfect thanks to employment becoming unstable. A couple of months prior one of my schools, the one that paid the most, had pulled the rug out from under me by giving my schedule to a teacher they'd contracted. Through happenstance that I knew the Director who did the hiring at one of the companies they'd sent me to, I kept my students there and he found me another. I had very good rapport with another teacher who'd hired me to work for her agency and she was instrument in keeping me alive. My schedule became one of mystery; I never knew what was happening one day to the next. My profession became mildly morbid as I lived in the hope someone would catch a cold and I'd get a chance to pick up more hours subbing. I advertised my availability on a website for teachers looking for employment and businesses looking for teachers. Around the time I'd signed the lease, thanks to that website, I was hired by an academy that gave me dependable hours to last through the end of the school year in June, plus benefits as if I were contracted. I finally had a lease and receipts for my payments that were legally accepted and I no longer had any ties to the orignal school, except for the deposit debate I intended to pick up with after I got settled. With the rent paid, I could move in at my convenience and my utilities'd be calculated from when I was officially situated. I was back in the more modern area only a few stops from where I'd first lived so, that wasn't so good. I was only a short distance from the metro and had easy access to the train station so, that was good. There were new ways for me to walk around the city I could connect with what I already knew, so that was very good. Believe it or not, although things were getting back on track and I finally had an apartment with a legal lease I could genuinely stay at long term, the two students I lived with were going to be the straw that ultimately broke the camel's back.

Taking a Break From the Drama & Stress, Not

Again, not exactly a chapter but I had a notion you might be a little curious about what could have possibly happened with my job. I thought we'd take a breather from thinking we were settled, meeting the real Lorine - Dr. South-Africa and Ms Rioja Hyde, having to split the scene with even more personal effects and that's with giving a considerable amount of things away, moving and moving again. At least this time around I lived out of my suitcases at Orlando's; all I had to do was zip 'em shut and go when the time came. The longer my stay the more I realized it was the way I should've been living from the start.

I went to work as usual, shared the usual greetings with who was in the office and went to my classroom to get it organized and prepare the lesson. The director came to the room to talk to me. He told me he had given my schedule to another teacher and I wasn't getting it back. I thought he had found someone to sub for me when I was visiting my son in Istanbul for his birthday – something that I told him was planned during my interview before he hired me; only a few days added to a weekend – so it made sense to me that if he was changing things around, I'd be getting other classes, something I wouldn't mind. He had me scheduled back to back lessons with no break between them, and before that started, I had to travel from a company where class ended at 4:30, to the school where class began at 4:30. I remained serene; I couldn't get upset because I was confused as to what exactly was going on. I asked questions and carried on conversation during which he suddenly exploded at me. I stood and watched, responded to his berating remarks, none of which implied I had done anything wrong as a teacher. I stated I had given up taking other assignments with other schools to accommodate him; he had me at companies and then at the academy itself to teach younger students. Nothing he was saying was about my teaching, but he didn't care whether or not I was a very good teacher (in a nutshell), he did what he did and I'm out. I continued to keep very calm and kept the discussion going for my own sake. We left one thing in the air about a company I worked for early in the morning with some advanced students. I went home in a state of shock. The rest of it you know. Neither I nor the Director of the company were getting a straight answer from him about whether or not I should teach there. The Director liked me; my students liked me and didn't want anyone else, so he told me to come to work. After that, I did some scrambling for teaching assignments.

I went to Istanbul with a ton of stuff for my son, that wasn't going to change. (I had one more stellar paycheck coming when I returned and after that, I didn't know.) I didn't say one word to him about what had happened.

Chapter 16: Two Oscars and A Grouch

At this apartment we chipped in for products like toilet paper, napkins, dish soap and supposedly, household cleaners. Once again and don't ask me why, my napkins were more interesting than the ones already there. After two or three days'd passed, Juan began mixing his refrigerated food with mine and after about two weeks'd passed both of them stalled buying toilet paper. Bottles of bleach I bought were used up quickly, where will forever remain a question, never replaced and didn't do the apartment good otherwise unless I was doing the cleaning. Paper towels I bought were being wasted. I found half a roll unrolled from the spindle into the trash. The stove burners weren't working right so I asked Juan about them. He wasted at least a dozen of my extra-long matches going through an explanation and then made a joke about how he needed to clean them. With this being my fifth residence, all I could think was "you've got to be kidding me". I had no doubt this place was different, there was no connection to the school here, Orlando had helped me find it and his heart was made of gold. Why was this happening - it felt like - déjà vu?

Nonetheless, it was necessary that small developing problems be nipped in the bud. I looked over the inside of the fridge. No one used the two crisper drawers, so I took them as my own leaving the other shelf space for my flat mates' use. Juan then started putting his food in the drawers. I removed his food, placed it on a shelf and put my name on both of the drawers with a Sharpie. Problem solved.

Completely stumped by the blatant wastefulness of household necessities I contributed, I put all my supplies in my cabinet instead of leaving them out in the open. I kept laundry products and bleach in my room along with a personal stash of toilet paper. The psychology used behind the toilet paper ploy was based on established truth: I am a girl; I need toilet paper (even with the luxury of a bidet). All they had to do was wait me out. They hadn't calculated their action (better to say lack of action) was a best way to kill my generous nature. A basic truth about many Spanish men is they won't do housework. I'd heard too many married female students and male students comment about this. The women expressed their frustration with the whole cultural flaw and the men were jocular about how they avoided it. Moms patronize their sons from the moment of birth from what I gathered and do everything for their precious darlings. Gay Spanish men are known for keeping house and I have to attest to Gonzalo's uniqueness. His mother must have taught him good cleaning techniques, (then again he's not from Madrid but from a different area in Spain so maybe it depends on the region and these issues are more Madrileño) which I saw him employ or reap the wrath of Mattia. Anyway, I even had a private stash of clothespins for the clothesline. New clothespins with the container got blown away from our balcony one gusty night. When it was windy, I'd bring the container in but my flat mates kept putting it back outside. Higher education surrounded me but no one was smart enough to consider second-to-top-floor wind velocity. I went out to rescue them one windy day but it was too late compliments of Juan hanging out a few things leaving them outside. Clothesline survivors I deemed property of the house. These things were minor glitches. Unbeknownst to me, there was another aberration awaiting:

Juan and Manuel were in the habit of using a chart that designated each person a room per week for cleaning, or they had just come up with the idea counting on me being the one most inclined toward domestic chores. Recalling the condition of the apartment when I'd first moved in, the latter might be truer than what they told me. In any case, it struck me as a good idea and I decided, rather than do all the work in one day, I'd clean as I go like I used to do when I'm at home. So when it was my week for bathroom, after showering I decided to get the chore of cleaning the toilet out of the way. I sprayed the cleaner around the bowl and grabbed the brush from its stand. To my horror and I mean absolute horror, the brush was completely covered in dried feces. It was so covered there was no possible way of cleaning it by washing the toilet with it and rinsing it off. Having been paralyzed, my imagination couldn't figure out how this had come to be. Germs, sickness and disease overrode all thought. I took the brush and holder and put them in a plastic bag. I put that bag in another, tied it tight and placed the package near the trash. I went to the store, bought a new set and put it in the bathroom. I was dropping a big hint. Little did I know the big hint was never going to be taken and the battle of the toilet brushes was going to occupy my remaining time there along with the battle of the kitchen counters and sink, the battle of the bathroom sink and the general battle of cleaning the room assigned to you. I would soon discover that after Juan cleaned there was no fresh scent. Things smelled dirty. One thing was becoming distressingly obvious: I was living with a very odd couple and both of them were real characters.

Chapter 17: There Once Was A Good One Who Went To England

Although he didn't always help the situation, Manuel was a little more conscientious about things than Juan. He noticed how clean the refrigerator was and admitted they should have taken care of it. I walked into the kitchen while he was there and he quickly pulled the refrigerator door open. "You cleaned it." "Yeah, it was too much for me. I was afraid to put my food in it, very scary. You know, germs, bacteria." He gazed at the shelves and made a droll joke "you mean germs were happy in my refrigerator before you came" while apologetically nodding his head at the food. "Yes, they were having a party in there." He let out a sigh. When I had to clean the kitchen counter after him, he tried to remember to at least brush crumbs into the sink. When he saw clean dishes, he knew I was behind it so he'd try to keep up with washing his. He was very bad about cleaning the room assigned him no matter which room it was. He'd check his name off the list without doing it. I was constantly on watch when it came to the bathroom and I cleaned regularly for my own sake. Still, I preferred Manuel's honesty about his lack of interest to whatever it was that Juan did that left things smelling dirty. He gave the allusion of having cleaned but in his hands products lost their effect. To this day I can't figure out how he did it. Juan's more self-centered than Manuel who is at least outgoing and personable. Manuel would talk about everything from sports to my job when we were both at the apartment together. He might have been the one to make things bearable enough that I'd have considered staying in Madrid another year. Having a couple of legal documents, the lease and my bank account verified by the lease, could possibly have been enough to get the government smiling in my direction. The academy (that treated me as if I were contracted) wanted me to return to Spain after the summer break and pick up teaching full time in the fall, but it happened Manuel's university decided to send him away to England for a summer of study leaving me with Juan. I didn't expect that I would find this distasteful enough to become a no-turning-back-point. After Manuel left, the apartment drama really took off:

I considered it a parting good deed when Manuel bought a multipack of double-roll toilet paper before he left. Mysteriously, with only Juan and I there, rolls kept diappearing from the cabinet. Sooner than it should have come it was Juan's turn and he bought a tiny four-pack of single-ply rolls. "You've got to be kidding me" was all I had. I'm a triple-ply multipack girl myself so for diplomacy and good faith I donated a few rolls to the cause and kept the remainder hidden away. A triple-ply roll disappeared the same day. That's it! Juan may have been using them for tissues but he could afford his own. I decided at that point to end community toilet paper. I kept what I bought in my room and carried a roll to the bathroom with me. On the other battlefronts:

Juan always left a mess in the kitchen. It was to such an extent I had to completely clean it in order to use it. We had a double sink which he filled with dishes, leaving them for whoever had the duty that week but I got into the habit of repiling them on one side to use the other or I'd just clean one side if it happened not to be compromised; in other words, I revamped the duty to whoever is cleaning the kitchen that week doesn't get to do your dishes. Take care of it yourself! It was similar with the bathroom sink only with whiskers. After he shaved he left a mess. He wasn't neat when using the toilet so I kept watch over toilet and floor around it which helped with the vigil over the brush. I watched over the tub and usually cleaned it before I stepped in for a shower. Juan enjoyed going to discos, dancing and drinking. I discovered he preferred hanging over the tub as opposed to aiming over the toilet seat to throw up what remained of his brains after an all-nighter. One morning as I was about to step in to shower, I noticed the tub smelled really bad; unusually bad. It took a few moments but I was able to determine what the aroma was. I decided to take precautions: just in case, clean first.

After mopping any floor the water was always left in the bucket to stagnate. I had to dump and rinse the bucket out if I wanted to use it so practically that helped the mop and bucket stay clean. We had a dining-room table dilemma: After Juan ate he never cleaned the table. He did remove his dishes to pile in the sink but he left the plastic tablecloth stained. He was a fan of pasta dishes with red sauce so there were dried and fresh dripped stains all over. He wasn't conscientious about cleaning off crumbs either. His lack of interest in our living environment amazed me. It seemed unnatural. As an Italian, I was taught to think of keeping house as something as important as keeping good relations between countries. I'd never consider cleaning an imposition; very simply and practically, it should be done. On a lesser battlefront: If I put an opened juice container in the refrigerator door Juan would take generous swigs from it. I tucked it away in the crisper drawer. He kept the freezer occupied to maximum capacity never considering anyone else who might want to use it. If I dared, I first had to find space, then seal and label everything to keep food safe from him. In fact, if it was necessary that I put something on a shelf in the fridge, I put my name on it and made sure I used Manuel's unoccupied shelves toward the back. I had to regularly restock the few general household supplies we shared. Juan used or pretended to use them, but in any case didn't replace any of them except the pine floor cleaner. I decided to keep track of his running tab of le comprado para la casa. Should he actually replace something I'd gladly deduct it. He had no idea I was keeping track of anything. Down the road when the list became impressive enough to make into a more formal document, I'd calculate in los otros domesticos, the extra housework I had to do in order to enjoy my new home.

Chapter 18: Hornlocking 101

The time finally came for the first split of the utilities bills. Juan matter-of-factly let me know he'd calculated from when I signed the lease and expected me to pay from that date. My time hadn't officially begun until the following Monday so he had to recalculate. While he was doing that so did I. I presented my figures to him and he responded with an undertone of regret, "your math is good, the figure is accurate." The total owed came to a whopping eight euro. Balanced against what he owed me, I should've given him less than two. Manuel'd told me "don't worry about money - when Juan wants it he'll let you know". Several days passed, he didn't ask for payment and I thought, maybe, he had some substance to him after all. I went as far as fantasizing that he was aware of what he wasn't replacing and what I was buying for the house. I couldn't have been more wrong about that one. He suddenly undiplomatically demanded money to the penny, about twenty centimos. I decided to just pay him and keep the fact of the bill I had started to myself. By not arguing I'd learn more about him, not that I wanted to but for the sake of survival. He obviously wasn't concerned with who bought what. Since I'd move there I'd been regaling my son with tales of Juan's lack of consideration and how his actions just floored me, but at his behest, "Ma, he's a guy. I'm sure there's nothing behind it, he just forgets about things. Remember when I was in Italy? I never remembered to buy stuff for the house, but when someone got something I'd just give them the euro for it. Just remind him. I'm sure everything will be ok", I started leaving reminder notes: "please dump the water after you mop - please clean off the counter - don't forget to buy paper towels - I bought the dish soap last time, your turn!" As for my son, what happened with him in Italy was true; he didn't act out of selfishness but more was going on with Juan than simple absentmindedness. He offered nothing and his concern was himself. For the most part Juan lived as if he were the only person in the apartment except for a couple of times he chose to point out to me we were alone together:

The only good thing about living with Juan, in spite of his aftermath, was that I seldom saw him. I began my day before he'd rise and came home before he'd get in. The occasions our paths would cross were when he wanted money. One Tuesday evening he happened to be in before me. He'd locked both locks on the door (as if he were in for the night), which is what told me he was already there. One of the first things Manuel'd told me was "only pull the door closed when you leave. Don't lock with the key. Sometimes the bolt sticks and it's hard to unlock. We never use it". Thanks a lot Juan. It took a while but I gained entry and headed to my room. (I know you're wondering why it took so long with Juan in the house. Didn't he hear me? Maybe he did, maybe he didn't over the radio he was listening too. Yes, I did knock and I was making enough clatter-clinking clatter trying to get everything open, but he didn't come to my assistance. I think it would be in keeping with diplomacy to call him a tool.) He was in the kitchen cooking. "What are you doing home! Early day for you!" At least tonight he wouldn't wake me with slamming doors and knocking into things passing from entryway, to bedroom, to bathroom, sometimes to kitchen and then back to bedroom, as he staggered in from who knows where. I'd figured out he was drunk a lot; I already knew he was thoughtless. "Yes, I got out of work early! I am lucky tonight." He was in an amiable mood so I joked with him about his job and what a nice, relaxing evening he was going to have. He looked me up and down with the imploring look, a common denominator among Spanish males, I've decided, Gonzalo had given me not so long ago. "Manuel is gone." "Yeah, he's in England having a good time I'm sure." "I got a letter from him. He has three flat mates and they get along well. He's happy." "Good for him! I'm glad." "We're alone in the house - you and me." He intensified the look but I didn't miss a beat. Keeping the conversation pleasant and objective I joked back "with your schedule and mine, the apartment has a lot of private time. Nothing changes for us." Smiling I tossed my head back slightly and calmly chuckled. The expression in his eyes changed and his smile faltered. He regrouped somewhat but the frown that followed told me I'd not given the anticipated response. I opened the fridge and grabbed a container of juice as I commented about the pasta dish he was cooking, how I noticed his fondness for pasta and salads and I could tell what he had for supper by the dishes he left in the sink. (No way was he going to take that hint.) I went back to my room leaving Juan and his poopy-faced expression in the kitchen. I mentally recapped what'd happened but found it hard to accept he was making an advance simply because of the age difference and although I've been told I look young, I know I don't look that young. What would a twenty-eight year old want with me? Seriously. My son was thirty-two and my daughter was twenty-five. There was always the possibility I was underestimating him the way I had Gonzalo, not taking actions seriously enough. It's said there's someone out there for everyone. I think mine gave up waiting and most likely married another woman; he certainly shouldn't be getting any younger. Was I in denial of signs?

One evening before Manuel'd left I'd come home and both of them were in the kitchen. There was a problem with the sink. Manuel was tinkering with the pipes as Juan looked on. I'd come in to get a snack and joked with them about Manuel the laborer and Juan the supervisor – he liked that one. As I stood there for a second watching the scene, Juan leaned in and whispered in my ear "we're using a condom". I hadn't been living at the apartment that long so Juan's remark was leaning toward off-center. Ignoring the heat from his sauce-stained breath that I feared was wilting my big curly hair, I dryly inquired, "is it working?" Manuel grunted, "we'll find out" as I turned and left. A moment later I heard water running and the two of them busting-out laughing. I guessed not musing about the outcomes. Anyway, about a week after the invitation of "we're alone", he made a second attempt toward another close encounter. He was home before I was again, had the door locked again but this time he was in the living room. I'd put my things in the bedroom and was en route to the bathroom when he burst out of the living room and stopped me as I was standing in the bathroom doorway, my arms full of toiletries. Why ever, we got on the subject of food. He eats a lot of meat. "I used to eat more meat but I don't eat as much anymore. I have more yogurt, fruits, nuts, veggies and fish. I love salads." "You must have a very strong body and be in very good shape." I got the look again with the slowly pondering-what-he-just-said smile. Now that I am in my fifties, I have a very realistic outlook on myself. I try to keep healthy and in shape. True. When a young man, let's say a twenty-eight year old ogles my body - I'm cautious. Maybe I should be more grateful. It did occur to me he might be poking fun at me. I held on to objectivity and glossed over his mention of my body, talked about how to stay healthy and changed the subject to what he was watching on TV. Was his favorite Spanish soap on or was this the night for his favorite dubbed American program? I told him I was looking forward to falling asleep reading a magazine and excused myself. I wasn't going to allow any more conversation along those lines whether he was serious or not. It would be easy enough to keep my distance. Back at the toilet brush ranch:

The latest replacement was becoming contaminated regularly. I tried to keep up by cleaning it when I used it cleaning and I also kept a stash of at least six or seven extra brushes in my bedroom closet. The day I bought them, the boy who worked at the family-run market marveled at the kind of house I lived in to need so many. "Kid, you don't know the half of it." I couldn't for the life of me figure out how Juan was managing it, didn't want to know which didn't prevent a couple of very gross thoughts from crossing my mind. Ugh! Things finally came to a head one fateful day opening a door to give him cleaning-the-toilet lessons: The replacement to the replacement that had been replaced fell victim (yes, three toilet-brushes in), resting in its cup-stand full of feces water. I took the set, doubled bagged it tight, shoved the package deep into the trash and went off to work thinking, don't ask me why, Juan would see another set had to be bought. What I saw when I came home for my afternoon break was outrageous:

I dropped my things in my room and hurried to the bathroom. I stopped dead in my tracks; all urges vanished. On the floor was the same set in its original contaminated condition. A chill ran through me that literally caused a shudder. I walked into the kitchen and gingerly peeked into the trash as if a snake were coiled to strike. There was no sign of the package I had shoved down in it. Horrified, I partially closed the kitchen door to check the hanging canvas bag we kept extra bags in. The two bags were crammed into the collection reeking of stool. I put on my rubber utility gloves, took out the bags plus others within too close for comfort proximity and put them all into a new plastic bag. I went to the bathroom, took the set and put it in with them. After tying everything tight, I took off my gloves, grabbed my keys, ran down the steps out to the dumpster, threw the bag in and went back inside. I tossed my keys on the bed and went to the bathroom. Before making lunch, I composed a note to Juan in English with Spanish subtitles. "I've thrown (expulsar) the brush and cup out. When it's that dirty, germs, (microbio, bacteria) disease and sickness (enfermadad) develop. Brushes and holders are easy to replace (sustituir) for less than two euro. I've bought (comprar algo) three (tres) of them so far." My train was late that evening so Juan had gotten home first. He made sure we crossed paths to talk about the note I'd left. First, he was offended that I had used Spanish because he was fluent in English. Down the road, when he'd try to take me for money I didn't owe him, he'd contradict that. Second, he played up how shocked he was when he went to the bathroom and the brush and cup weren't there (although I had a stash of extras, I didn't have a set with a cup – I'd have to pick up another of those). I seized that moment and interjected a lesson in cleaning the toilet. Remaining fully dressed (you'd better believe it; I was taking a risk doing this), I mimed pooping, flushing and spraying cleaner around the rim. I showed him how to rinse the brush off by genuinely flushing once then twice and demonstrated shaking the excess water off the brush before putting back in its holder. Mission accomplished. He wasn't happy about the lesson either but I kept smiling. "See now - no more problems. Cleaning is easy."

Chapter 19: All's Temporarily Quiet On The Madrileno Front Except For My Deposit

I kept a watchful eye over the brush and was pleased this one had a longer shelf life than any of the others. Still, my mind was not at peace. The thought "once the school year is over, leave Madrid" wouldn't go away. I knew I didn't want to continue living at the apartment with Juan. Manuel was nice though sloppy but I didn't really want to clean up after him. The price was right. I could afford to pay three months' rent to cover the summer, arrange with the realtor to go away and return in the fall to teach another year. I'd have to have a lock installed on my bedroom door. On the brighter side, Orlando's apartment could become available again or I could take the opportunity offered me for an apartment share with one of the teachers who worked at the academy. I'd be living nearer to the school in Tres Cantos, where it was located. Neither of those thoughts sparked any motivation. My sense of adventure, my determination, the excitement of new life opening up, were nowhere to be found. I put thoughts aside; let them wage against each other in the back of my mind, while I focused on a loose end or two.

The school that'd invited me on my Spanish Adventure had no intention of helping me get my deposit refunded. I'd stopped in a few days after their meeting with the agent and was told, "what she says is different than what you say. If you want us to help you you'll have to prove everything. Find emails and phone records." Nancy's other business partner, Lucy, waxed philosophical about how I should just give up on the money and wasn't it about time I moved on. Nancy was in complete denial of her interference with my living situation. Easy enough I went through all communications and forwarded more than they asked of me.
I kept up arguing with the agent who admitted her guilt to me in an email written in Spanish, which she assumed I wouldn't understand. (She began her communication by mocking my educational background and expertise as a real teacher. If I were actually standing close to her, she might have grabbed handfuls of hair and

started pulling. I couldn't muster up much in the name of emotion about it; I was that worn. As I read through I thought. "Well, there's my confirmation.") After I thanked her for the reveal-all soliloquy, she stopped writing and the school stopped talking. Bullying remarks about what I should let go of and give up ceased. Windows were locked and shades were drawn. It irked me that I was going to lose money; fortunately not a large amount but that wasn't the point. Sometime after this, Nancy and her partner happened through my barrio (neighborhood) and we bumped into each other on the street. "We were just thinking 'hey – we know her'- Lorine stopped by and dropped off things you'd left when you moved." I stood there for a moment thinking "who?" and then realized "oh, Lorine - better I don't block her out - I should thank them for reminding me". I said, "That was a while ago. I didn't leave anything I wanted or missed." "Well, what do you want us to do with them? There's an interesting assortment." I ended the conversation with "If there's good toilet paper use it with my blessing" and continued on. Nancy's partner gave a started sigh, the two of them stood there momentarily disoriented and then continued on their way. I waited a week then followed up with emails about why, after I'd proved my case I hadn't received the small amount that was owed me. There was no response at all but before that last ruse I'd decided to drop it anyway.

The final decision to leave Madrid came to me in a similar way the decision to leave New York did when my kids were much younger and I was in my second bad marriage. Someone said something that found its way through the pain, confusion and guilt. "If you can't do any good in your situation, it's ok to change it." Simple enough but I couldn't see it on my own. I packed up two young children, somewhere between nine to thirteen suitcases and moved to the mid-west to start a new life. What was taking place at my fifth residence wasn't as earth shattering but it wasn't good either. My year had been trying and I was exhausted. The government was cracking down on illegals as the global financial crisis was taking hold in Spain. Unemployment was rising and I'd been forewarned by a teacher who'd hired me, one who was not only my colleague but my friend, she wouldn't be able to keep me as busy as she'd like if at all because her agency was only going to employ contracted teachers. Things all around were changing for the worse but none of that actually mattered. I knew I didn't want to continue living where I was. The pros of cost, location, convenience and even Orlando couldn't outweigh a year's worth of cons. Travel was becoming restricted and I didn't want any more high stress or risk being confined to Madrid. I knew it wasn't necessary to weigh anything against anything. My time was finished. Originally Juan and Manuel had insisted I stay very long term – something that should have sent my soul singing. Continuing with the academy that wanted me to come back in the fall, I could've afforded the rent. No one knew that but me. I came up with a story, partially true; that because of the crisis there wouldn't be enough work for me so I couldn't stay. "The deposit will be the last month's rent and you can use the rest toward utilities." Juan waxed anal about how he should get at least one month's notice. I was telling him, wasn't I? I bought a plane ticket and with more than a month to spare, officially posted a notice on the refrigerator I was leaving the twenty-eighth of June.

Chapter 20: Last Call

It's funny when we make decisions that change things we sense something in the air. A light breeze blows though we're standing inside with no windows open. There's a gentle stir of adrenaline that freshens, clears and frees the atmosphere. After posting my note my sense of adventure stirred and my mind went into business mode as if I were in charge of an office being restructured. I had a new gun to my head in the name of downsizing. All things must go! Well, maybe not all things. I'd most likely keep some underwear and socks but with the weight limit set at twenty-two kilos, roughly forty-five pounds, about three-quarters of what I'd accumulated had to be left behind. I'd decided to head to Istanbul to see my son, so there would be gifts for him and my daughter. As I looked around my room envisioning what could go, I imagined office bustling and people boxing supplies for shipping. I grabbed a Desigual handled bag and began folding clothes into it although it wasn't long before I had to stop so I could catch the train to get back to work. I felt a peacefulness having started the wheels turning for a new beginning, which helped take away some of the sting from what I would have to lose.

The apartment drama was at a temporary lull. I'd managed to keep thwarting Juan's attempts at communication by missing running into him, bless our schedules, as I kept occupied with sorting who was going to get what and what was going to go where. As a last ditch effort though, he showed up one Saturday afternoon, "damn, what's he doing here?", to cook himself dinner. I'd strategically planned my walk like I always did on the weekend to arrive home long after he was gone. He snapped on the dance-music radio station in the kitchen as he occupied himself making yet another pasta and red sauce dish. It'd be soon enough he'd be able to throw sauce on the walls - I wouldn't be there to care. I was in the living room watching a dubbed movie so I closed the door in order to hear. In he walked with his filled bowl, sat down and proceeded to ask questions about the program. I wasn't interested in speaking to him at all, so politely I grunted and h'mmmd short answers letting my attention drift back to the TV. He eventually fell into a perplexed silence, ate and closed the door quietly behind him when he left. In the background I heard him getting ready to go back out and I opened the door again when I was alone. Yes! (Even though, victory wasn't going to be mine quite yet.) After this we didn't speak to each other much. The silence that was growing was releasing as co-existence fell into a comfortable routine. We shared nothing and I focused on restructuring:

In this part of town, I had to pick and choose where I could place things for the needy. The community was distant when it came to the poor and the refugees. I discovered in what ways when I'd left a bag of shoes next to a dumpster just outside my building. I kept tabs on things as a rule, went out to check to see if they'd been taken a little later on and found they had been separated, one of the pair placed in the dumpster and one left in the bag. I went back, dug everything out and put the bag in a different spot. When I checked again it'd been taken as a whole. Special odds and ends I shared with my students and co-workers. My youngest students thought Christmas'd come early. Each day that brought us all closer to the end of the school year and summer vacation we held raffles. Sometimes I'd spread things across the table for first come, first served and say "help yourself - always remember to keep getting to class on time!" My older students chose books to test their english prowess and I left most of the totes, extra umbrellas and reference guides in the office. A few bags-full were made for teachers who were staying behind to tough Madrid out a little longer. I was going to stay with Orlando the weekend I was leaving for easier access to the airport and to be in Sol one last time. He'd get the bulk of what would stay behind. (I really did accumulate a lot of stuff.) Life was moving on, stress was moving out and I looked forward to my peace settling back into its rightful place as my center; however,

One night, about two weeks before I was going to depart, Juan decided to disturb my sleep to talk about final bills for the utilities. I was so groggy it was a wonder I could stand up, which he found amusing. I leaned against my bedroom doorway for support and he laughed "were you alseep? Ha-ha-ha. Come into the livingroom." I was visibly annoyed but that didn't deter his purpose. He droned on about calculations and demanded that I pay one more month's rent. I wasn't that groggy, so I refused reminding him that my deposit was going toward the last month's rent and the balance toward lingering utilities. He told me the realtor wasn't going to accept the deposit as the rent; I had to pay him the money and she would fully refund my deposit in a week's time, which made absolutely no sense at all. He also tried to charge me for a utility I'd never seen a bill for since I'd been there saying it might finally come when I was gone. I staggered between living room and bedroom to retrieve my calendar, receipt book and finally my cell phone. I showed him everything I'd payed, that there weren't any extra charges like he was talking about and I wasn't paying any more rent. Juan suddenly lost his fluency. He didn't understand anything I was saying in Spanish or English anymore and muttered "realtor - no english" with a smug grin expecting me to hand him cash as my only recourse. I snapped open my cell and called Orlando. Juan's attitude suddenly changed and his memory began to return. He kept repeating "it's not necessary to call anyone" but sorry Juan, too late now. When Orlando answered I relayed the conversation and handed over my cell. After talking to Orlando, Juan handed it back. Orlando told me I had nothing to worry about, the realtor had no problem with using my deposit to cover the last month's rent. "Call me if he gives you a hard time about anything else." Undaunted, Juan then tried to press me for future utilities. I couldn't believe what I was hearing and was very annoyed that all the activity had me fully awake. I made him an offer to shut him up. "When will you pay me?" "I don't know Juan. I have to go to the bank. Maybe Friday." "OK. I'll be here so you can pay me." I gathered up my things and went back to my room. I wasn't happy with what had happened and it didn't sit with me that I should pay him anything. I didn't owe him anything. He had taken me for as much as he could by not contributing to household goods, using my supplies when he could get away with it and causing me extra housework because of his self-centeredness and inconsideration. I didn't think it monumental enough to call Orlando back about; somehow I was going to fix it not to give him one more centimo. It took me a while to fall back to sleep but by the time I did I'd decided to use the tally of things he owed and draw up a bill.

Chapter 21: We'll Always Have Madrid (Here's To Not Lookin' At You Anymore)

I wasn't as tired as I thought I'd be when I woke the next morning. Although what'd happened troubled me I had a renewed sense of purpose about accomplishing my goal. I wasn't sure how I was going to pull it off exactly but I knew Juan wasn't getting any more money from me. Friday rolled around and he was already home when I got there. My stomach twisted as I un-double bolted the door. I was greeted with dance music blaring from his room and a sickly artificial fruity fragrance emanating from his ajar door. I went to my room and changed while a flood of thoughts ran through my mind. "He always closes his door. I wonder what's up - maybe an invitation to pay... what's that smell? Artificial and cheap, just like him." I listened by my door and knew he was still involved with himself so I hurried to the bathroom and then the kitchen. I made sure I had everything I wanted in the name of juice, bottled water and snacks so I wouldn't have to leave my room until after he was gone. Of course, there was always the possibility he'd bang on my door and demand money. From the sounds of things he was getting ready for another all-nighter. I hurried back to my room, got comfortable on the bed and began drafting a bill.

I decided on bi-lingual in case of another lapse of fluency without the least bit of concern whether or not I offended him. After the rough draft was completed, I edited, reworded, decided on what got Spanish emphasis and realigned the spacing. I wanted to leave room for additions to and – to be fair - deductions. My finished product looked good, so all that was left was to verify how I'd stated everything in Spanish.
I started reading a magazine after that to bide the time. Juan'd turned off the music and was pacing around the apartment. I felt confident and ready for any argument he might give me. Everything got quiet and I heard a door close. I stopped reading and listened but didn't hear a sound. I peeked out my door. The place was completely dark, the door to his room was closed but not clicked shut which is the sign he'd gone out. I checked to be sure and came out of hiding to

watch TV in the livingroom. (So far, so good.) I watched movies then went to bed. When I woke the next morning, Juan's door still wasn't closed tight. I cautiously pushed it open with one finger and peeked in. He wasn't there and I mused should I dare hope he'd be gone for the weekend! When I got up for work Monday he still hadn't returned. Works for me. Now I had the chance to give the bill the once over before I presented it.

Mondays and Wednesdays I had two advanced conversation students. I'd been regaling them with my escapades of finding an apartment in Madrid and the drama that accompanied them. They loved hearing my stories and were more than interested in holding conversations about them. That Monday I'd planned to continue with "the demand for money when I was half asleep", and "waiting out the enemy as I compiled the list of charges". I was going to let them proof read my Spanish making it a lesson in transitioning language. I knew they'd love the challenge and I'd get more of the inside scoop on speaking like a Madrileño. I'd titled my document "Maggie's Losses".
They liked the layout: first I wrote everything out in bulleted sentences with Spanish subtitles - clothespins (pinzas) 2 pks lost (perdidos) - toilet brushes (bano cepillo) 1 set plus (y) replaced 4 (sustituir) - bleach (leija) 5 bottles (botellas) and so on. Then I made a tally with costs of each. I made another bulleted list of extra housekeeping, my otros domesticos: cleaning (limpiar) counter (cocina mostrador?) and tables (las mesas) every day 2 mes - mopping (fregar) bathroom floor around toilet after Juan (3 mes). I had five extra housekeeping jobs total. I concluded by adding the charge for housekeeping - bajo economico para 3 mesas (very inexpensive for three months of work) - with the charges for la comprado para la casa (cleaning supplies). After deducting my wages, Juan owed me money! As a final salutation I wrote "Eres desconsiderado. Me gusta mudorse (gambiar direccione) – Maggie. In other words: "You're very inconsiderate. I'm glad I'm moving". My students told me he wouldn't pay me but he also wasn't going to press me for any more money - his pride was going to be stung which was the end result I'd wanted. When I got home that night he

still wasn't back. (Zippidee do dah zipideeay, my oh my how many wonderful days!) I'd made a copy of the bill and posted it on the fridge tucking the original away with the lease. He didn't return until Wednesday. When I got home that night the house was deserted but I knew he'd seen the bill. It'd been moved from it's spot. Up until I left, he avoided me.

The weekend of my departure rolled around and I spent Friday and part of Saturday carting suitcases to Orlando's. Juan was away for the weekend again - yay! As I was taking my last piece of luggage, I took the bill from under the refrigerator magnet and put it on one of the mini kitchen tables with the keys on top of it. I checked around to make certain I wasn't leaving anything behind although I knew I got it all. I stepped into the hallway and pulled the door shut. Adios!

Chapter 22: Epitaph

El Condor Pasa

I can't say El Condor Pasa was running through my mind as I took my last train ride with the last suitcase to Orlando's. I'll always have fond memories of the rush-hour musician who played it on the metro one day instead of The Sound of Silence, a favorite number usually played to death for traveling entertainment in the hopes of a contribution; I've heard it on pipes and guitar always with a pre-recorded accompaniment. When I recognized it, I shared some centimos. Tough luck Juan!

After getting situated - for the last time - I wandered around the town center picking up the last few things for my son. I looked forward to seeing him and living in Istanbul for a while. Knowing teaching'd be slow over the summer, I'd planned a side excursion to the states to visit my daughter. The day of my flight, I decided to treat myself to a ride in a taxi instead of carting suitcases to the station, then on and off the train. I was worn on so many levels, and wasn't feeling tough enough for one final Herculean demonstration of strength; if Madrid hadn't noticed by now, it was never going to see it. After the driver unloaded my luggage at the airport he tried to con me into letting him keep the change to add to his tip. The charge to the airport, twenty-five euro, included the gratuity and still does to this day as far as I know. As I walked away tugging suitcases behind me while shaking my head after getting all my change, I gave my year's worth of stress back to Madrid. "Madrid, You can keep it" I thought, "I don't have to deal with it anymore". My luggage was overweight, which I was prepared for. When I checked in the airline assistant timidly told me the news. I said, "Yes. I know. I'm leaving so everything has to come. What do I owe you – about 140?" In appreciation of my calmness and willingness to pay without arguing, I'm guessing, but for whatever reason, I was given a considerable discount. Added to the cost of my ticket, the trip was still inexpensive. At the window where I had to pay, I received smiles and well wishes for a pleasant flight.

I had never been interested in seeing Spain much less teaching there, which meant nothing had changed my outlook in that respect, but I wouldn't trade my experience or the friends I made for the world. Had I remained another year, I'd be quite fluent.

As the plane reached altitude, I relaxed.

www.ingramcontent.com/pod-product-compliance
Lightning Source LLC
Chambersburg PA
CBHW051842020726
47502CB00005B/1910